Th

Letter

by

Kathi Daley

I want to thank the very talented Jessica Fischer for the cover art.

I so appreciate Bruce Curran, who is always ready and willing to answer my cyber questions, Jayme Maness, who helps out with my book clubs and special events, and Peggy Hyndman, for helping sleuth out those pesky typos.

Thank you to Pam Curran, Vivian Shane, Nancy Farris, and Darla Taylor for submitting recipes.

And, of course, thanks to the readers and bloggers in my life, who make doing what I do possible.

Thank you to Randy Ladenheim-Gil for the editing.

And finally I want to thank my sister Christy for always lending an ear and my husband Ken for allowing me time to write by taking care of everything else.

Books by Kathi Daley

Come for the murder, stay for the romance.

Zoe Donovan Cozy Mystery:

Halloween Hijinks
The Trouble With Turkeys
Christmas Crazy
Cupid's Curse
Big Bunny Bump-off
Beach Blanket Barbie
Maui Madness
Derby Divas
Haunted Hamlet
Turkeys, Tuxes, and Tabbies
Christmas Cozy
Alaskan Alliance
Matrimony Meltdown
Soul Surrender
Heavenly Honeymoon
Hopscotch Homicide
Ghostly Graveyard
Santa Sleuth
Shamrock Shenanigans
Kitten Kaboodle
Costume Catastrophe
Candy Cane Caper
Holiday Hangover
Easter Escapade
Camp Carter
Trick or Treason
Reindeer Roundup

Tj Jensen Paradise Lake Mysteries by Henery Press:

Pumpkins in Paradise
Snowmen in Paradise
Bikinis in Paradise
Christmas in Paradise
Puppies in Paradise
Halloween in Paradise
Treasure in Paradise
Fireworks in Paradise
Beaches in Paradise – *June 2018*

Whales and Tails Cozy Mystery:

Romeow and Juliet
The Mad Catter
Grimm's Furry Tail
Much Ado About Felines
Legend of Tabby Hollow
Cat of Christmas Past
A Tale of Two Tabbies
The Great Catsby
Count Catula
The Cat of Christmas Present
A Winter's Tail
The Taming of the Tabby
Frankencat
The Cat of Christmas Future
The Cat of New Orleans – *February 2018*

Seacliff High Mystery:

The Secret
The Curse
The Relic
The Conspiracy
The Grudge
The Shadow
The Haunting

Sand and Sea Hawaiian Mystery:

Murder at Dolphin Bay
Murder at Sunrise Beach
Murder at the Witching Hour
Murder at Christmas
Murder at Turtle Cove
Murder at Water's Edge
Murder at Midnight

Writers' Retreat Southern Seashore Mystery:

First Case
Second Look
Third Strike
Fourth Victim
Fifth Night – *January 2018*

Rescue Alaska Paranormal Mystery:
Finding Justice

A Tess and Tilly Mystery:
The Christmas Letter

Road to Christmas Romance:
Road to Christmas Past

Chapter 1

Wednesday, December 6

My name is Tess Thomas. I live with my dog, Tilly, in White Eagle, Montana, a small town with a big heart nestled in the arms of the Northern Rocky Mountains. I work for the United States Postal Service, delivering mail to the residents of this close-knit community where, more often than not, the folks you grow up with are the same ones you're destined to grow old with.

"Morning, Tess; morning, Tilly," Hap Hollister greeted us as we delivered not only his mail, but the muffins Hattie Johnson had asked me to drop off when Tilly and I had stopped by Grandma Hattie's Bakeshop earlier that morning.

"Morning, Hap." I handed the tall, thin man with snow-white hair a stack of envelopes, as well as the brown paper bag in which Hattie had packed the muffins.

"Pumpkin?" Hap asked.

"Cranberry. Hattie wanted me to assure you they're fresh."

I watched as Hap peeked in the bag. "How's Hattie's arthritis this morning?"

"She seems to be having a good day. You can go by later and ask her yourself." Odd fact about Hap and Hattie: They used to be married, but they separated a few years ago and moved into separate residences, but now they date.

"I'll do that. Hattie and I are planning to take in a movie at the cinema in Kalispell this evening if the snow holds off. Guess I should firm up a time for us to meet."

"You might want to have a backup plan. With those dark clouds overhead, I have a feeling the storm's going to roll in before nightfall. The Community Church has bingo on Wednesdays, if you can't make it to Kalispell."

"Thanks. I'll keep that in mind. It's been hard to find date-night activities since the cinema in town decided to shut down during the winter."

I slipped my mailbag off my shoulder, being careful not to catch my long, curly brown hair in the strap. "I heard there's a group who want to use the space for community events during the winter, though it seems like a lot of folks in the area have an abundance of ideas but are short on follow-through."

"Sounds about right."

I picked up a stack of Christmas CDs Hap had displayed at the front of the home and hardware store Hap owned and operated and began to sort through them. I know that in the age of iTunes, iPods, and smartphones, CDs are a bit outdated, but if you knew the folks of White Eagle, you'd know a lot of them were pretty outdated as well.

"If nothing works out for tonight you could postpone date night until Friday," I suggested. "We have the tree lighting and there's a holiday special at the diner."

"Nope." Hap shook his head. "That won't do at all. Our agreement clearly states that Hattie is to cook dinner for me every Sunday after church, as well as on the seven major holidays, and in return, I'm to take her out on a proper date I plan and pay for every Wednesday as well as every other Saturday."

I paused and looked at Hap. "Has it ever occurred to you and Hattie to set aside this experiment you're engaged in and get back together full time, like everyone knows you should?"

"Sure." Hap nodded but didn't elaborate.

I wanted to say more, but it really wasn't any of my business, so I set the CDs back in the bin and prepared to leave. "Tilly and I should get going if we want to stay ahead of the storm. Got anything outgoing?"

"Actually, I do." Hap set the muffin he'd been nibbling on on the napkin Hattie had provided. "Just give me a minute to fetch it."

Tilly and I wandered over to the potbellied stove to warm up a spell while we waited for Hap. It wasn't easy being a mail carrier in White Eagle, with subzero temperatures and seasonal snow to contend with. But White Eagle was our home, and as far as Tilly and I were concerned, we wouldn't trade it for all the tropical breezes or big-city amenities in the world.

"Here you go." Hap placed a stack of white envelopes on the counter next to a small pile of fishing supplies.

"You planning on doing some fishing?" I asked as I picked up the envelopes.

"A group of us are fixing to enter the old-timers' ice fishing competition at the Winter Carnival." The Winter Carnival in White Eagle was held every year between Christmas and New Year's. "I haven't been fishing since last year's carnival, so I figured I'd better go through my supplies."

"I know the teams are made up of four men. Harley Newsome passed away this year. Have you found a replacement?"

"I spoke to Pike and he said he'd be happy to fill in."

Pike Porter was White Eagle's oldest resident at ninety-two.

"Are you sure that's a good idea?" I asked.

"Man's old, not dead. He said he wanted to do it and I'm inclined to let him."

I supposed Hap had a point, but I worried about Pike walking around on the ice. Once again, however, what he did was none of my business, so I slipped Hap's outgoing mail into my bag without a word. "I really should get a move on. I'll talk to you tomorrow."

"Have you been by Rita's place?" Hap asked as I turned to the door.

"No, not yet." Rita Carson was the local florist.

"I want to send Hattie a rose. Rita said she'd be getting in a shipment today." Hap handed me a twenty-dollar bill. "If you don't mind passing this along, I'd greatly appreciate it."

"No problem." I slid the currency into my pocket.

"Tell Rita to pick out a good one."

"I will, and I'll make sure she delivers it today."

"Thanks, Tess. See you tomorrow."

I pulled the collar of my jacket around my neck as Tilly and I left Hap's store. There were snow flurries in the air, which I knew would precede the storm that approached from the far side of the mountain.

I looked at the red envelope at the top of the pile. "Looks like Pike has a letter today."

Tilly barked once in reply. Pike Porter wasn't only one of Tilly's favorite people, he was one of my favorite people as well.

"Let's finish the rest of the route and circle around toward Pike's last so we can sit and chat for a spell. I want to hear all about his plans for the ice fishing tournament."

Tilly must have figured that was a fine idea because she continued down Main Street, passing the alley that led to Pike's tiny cabin, which shared a lot with Pike's Place, the local saloon, which Pike had once owned but had sold.

The next stop on our journey was Sisters' Diner, the café my mom, Lucy Thomas, owned with my aunt, Ruthie Turner. My mom and Aunt Ruthie had decided to buy the diner after my dad passed away and Mom realized she would need to find a way to support herself. Ruthie had worked as a cook for the diner's previous owner, who'd expressed a desire to retire to a warmer climate, so the two sisters had pooled their savings and been making a go of the restaurant ever since.

The wreath someone had hung on the door shifted to the side as Tilly and I entered the entryway of the warm, friendly building. I had to smile as a decorative Rudolph with a flashing nose welcomed diners while "Frosty the Snowman" played in the background.

"I've got Christmas cards." I held up several colorful envelopes as I entered the main dining area.

"Oh, good." Mom clapped her hands in delight. Mom and Aunt Ruthie had come up with the idea of soliciting Christmas cards from customers who had dined with them throughout the year. They planned to hang the cards on the back wall after sorting them by general geographic location. It was a cute idea that would not only brighten the place but would demonstrate the fact that customers who stopped by Sisters' Diner represented visitors from every state, as well as many countries around the world.

"Oh, look," Mom said, waving her arms in the air so her red curls bounced up and down. "We have two from Nevada, one from Florida, four from Utah, and one from Florence, Italy."

"Today was a good haul," I agreed. "And the wall is looking really nice. If this idea continues to catch on, you may need to dedicate two walls to the project next year."

"I've been thinking the same thing." Mom grinned. "In fact, with the abundance of international cards that have arrived in the past week, I'm considering changing the theme of this year's tree from Homespun Christmas to Christmas Around the World."

"That would be fun. Maybe you could find ornaments representing all the countries you get cards from, like the Eiffel Tower and the Leaning Tower of Pisa."

"Exactly. Did you notice whether Millie had her novelty ornaments out yet?" Millie Martin owned a home and decorating store at the other end of the row of mom-and-pop shops lining the town's main thoroughfare.

"I didn't notice them when I stopped by to deliver her mail, but I wasn't looking for them either. I guess you can call to ask her. If nothing else, she may be able to special order the kinds of ornaments you're looking for."

"That's a good idea."

"So, what are we talking about?" Aunt Ruthie asked after she finished ringing up the customer she'd been dealing with and joined us.

"Ornaments from around the world," Mom answered.

"Did you ask Tess if Millie has her specialty ornaments out?" Ruthie asked.

"She did and I hadn't noticed," I answered in my mom's stead. "She did have baby's first Christmas ornaments displayed near the counter if you want to send something to Johnny."

"The baby won't be born until January, so baby's first Christmas would technically be next year," Aunt Ruthie pointed out. "Still, I'd like to send something special because they're having a girl. I'm hoping they'll name her after me. She's my first granddaughter, you know."

"I'm sure Johnny will take your request into consideration when it comes time to name his daughter." I paused and glanced out the window. "Storm is coming; I'd best be on my way." I turned and looked at my mom. "Dinner on Sunday?"

"Of course, dear. I'll make a pot roast."

Tilly and I left the diner, but not before Aunt Ruthie slipped Tilly a bite of something she'd smuggled from the kitchen. I tried to dissuade Ruthie from feeding Tilly table scraps, but she liked to be sure those who came into the diner were well fed whether they be the customers she served or the four-legged visitors, like Tilly, who were only passing by.

The flurries that had been lingering throughout the day were beginning to intensify by the time Tilly and I made our way to the far end of town and crossed the street to start back toward the gazebo, where I'd left my Jeep. I usually liked to say hi to those I served, but given the weather, I realized I might want to speed things up a bit if I didn't want to get caught in a whiteout.

I managed to stick with the plan while delivering mail to Pete's Pets, Sue's Sewing Nook, the Moosehead Bar and Grill, Mel's Meat Locker, and even Rita's shop, Coming Up Daisies, but the moment I entered the Book Boutique, my best friend Bree Price's bookstore, I knew I'd lose my momentum.

"Please tell me you're coming to book club tonight," Bree said the moment Tilly and I entered the cheerily decorated store.

"Tilly and I will be there," I confirmed over the sound of Christmas carols.

"Good." Bree nervously ran her hands down the sides of her dark green angora sweater dress in a gesture I had come to recognize as the prelude to her relaying information she knew I might not want to hear.

"Is there something on your mind?" I asked.

"No." Bree shook her head, but I noticed she was trying hard not to look me in the eye.

"Are you sure?" I asked persuasively.

"Nothing's wrong, but there are some new members joining us tonight. I figured I should let you know so you could wear something nice."

I frowned. "Nice?"

Bree tucked a lock of her perfectly straight, waist-length blond hair behind one ear. "I just figured you might want to make a good first impression because both new members are male, single, and gorgeous. Based on what I know of them, either would make a good match for you."

I lifted one brow. "We've discussed this. I don't do blind dates. Not for anyone and not for any reason."

"It's not a blind date," Bree insisted. "It's just book club, but it seems silly not to put forth a little effort with your appearance. You're going to be twenty-eight on your next birthday. Don't you think it's time to settle down?"

"If by settle down you mean get married, no. Tilly and I are quite happy living on our own. You promised you'd stop with all the matchmaking and I expect you to keep your promise."

"I know," Bree replied. "I just want you to be as happy as Donny and me."

Donny Dunlap was my ex, who I'd dumped after I realized he paid a lot more attention to Bree than he ever paid to me. I know Bree felt bad about basically stealing my guy, but the truth of the matter was, I was never really in to Donny all that much, and I was fine with the way things had worked out. Still, Bree, being Bree, wasn't going to fully enjoy her relationship with Donny until I met and fell in love with someone she felt was perfect for me.

"Storm's coming so I need to get going. I'll be at book club, but only if you promise to lay off the matchmaking."

Bree paused.

"Promise me."

"Okay," Bree grudgingly agreed. "Have you been to the police station?"

"No, not yet. Why?"

"Can you drop this book off for your brother? I told him I'd deliver it, but you're going to be stopping in anyway, so…"

"Yeah." I reached out a hand. "I'll make sure Mike gets it."

I had just left the Book Boutique and Tilly and I were heading to our next stop when a bright green sports car whizzed by, splashing slush on both of us. "Damn it all to hell," I said before I could suppress the curse. "There's no way Fantasia didn't do that on purpose."

Tilly shook the slush from her fur and barked in agreement.

Fantasia Wade was a twenty-eight-year-old gold digger and former classmate of mine who'd recently married seventy-nine-year-old Austin Wade, the oldest son of one of the town founders and one of the richest men in town. In the year the pair had been married, Fantasia had managed to burn through an impressive amount of his money, which left me wondering when Austin would wise up and put his young bride on a budget.

Given the fact that I had slush running down my cheek, I turned around and headed back to the bookstore, where I knew Bree would let me clean up in her bathroom.

"What on earth happened to you?" Bree asked when I walked back into her store just a minute after having left.

"Fantasia."

Bree rolled her eyes. "Talk about letting money go to your head. Now that she's married to Austin Wade she seems to think the rules of common courtesy don't apply to her."

"She always has been full of herself. I'll just be a minute."

I tried not to let my anger boil over as I washed my face and used a paper towel to wipe the dirt from my jacket. There were just some people who were born thinking they were better than everyone else and Fantasia was one of them. Of course, the fact that she was drop-dead gorgeous seemed to fuel her superiority complex. It's hard to tell someone who was head cheerleader, homecoming queen, and the most popular girl in school that she's no better than you and make her believe it.

Tilly and I tried to put our little incident with Queen Wade behind us as we finished our route. By the time I'd made my way back to the starting point, where I'd left my Jeep, the sky had darkened. I figured Tilly and I would just drive over to Pike's, so I loaded her in the cargo area, made a U-turn, and headed back to the cabin where White Eagle's oldest resident lived. My route had taken longer than I'd planned, so I wouldn't have as long to chat with Pike as I'd like, but he only received mail a couple of times a month, so when we had a reason to stop in, we generally took it.

"Pike," I called as I rapped on the door.

When there was no answer, Tilly used a paw to scratch at the door.

"Pike, it's Tess and Tilly," I called again.

Still no answer.

I looked down at Tilly. "I guess he's out."

Tilly barked and scratched at the door again. Normally, Tilly wasn't quite so insistent, so I knocked one more time for good measure before slipping the letter under the door and turning away to head back to the Jeep.

Tilly remained at the door rather than following. "Come along, Tilly. Pike's not home."

Tilly barked.

"I know you were looking forward to a visit, but we'll have to come back another day. Maybe tomorrow."

Tilly lay down on the front stoop as if to communicate that she would wait.

"It's snowing and it's almost dark. We can't just stand here waiting for Pike to come home. We still need to make dinner and get cleaned up before book club. Now come along."

Tilly is a sweet and obedient dog who always responds to my requests, so I wasn't sure why she was being so stubborn now. I walked back over to the stoop to give her a gentle shove in the right direction when I heard a tiny sound coming from the other side of the door. I knocked once more but still got no answer. Tilly barked and continued scratching at the door.

"Is Pike in trouble? Do you think we should check on him?"

Once again, Tilly barked.

I reached for the knob and turned it. It was unlocked, so I pushed the door open.

The first thing I noticed was that a pile of fishing supplies that must have at one time been on the table were now on the floor. The next thing was a tiny orange-striped kitten was tangled up in a piece of fishing line, which had gotten caught on a nearby table leg. "I suppose you're responsible for Pike's fishing supplies being on the floor."

"Meow."

"Hang on. I have a knife in my Jeep. I'll get it and cut you free."

Tilly stayed with the kitten while I ran back to get the knife. The poor baby was tangled up pretty good. I was going to need to work carefully to get him free without injuring him. It took a good fifteen minutes to finally work him loose, but eventually, I was able to gather him up in my hands. I noticed the poor thing had a nasty-looking cut on one leg.

"Looks like we'll need to stop by to visit Doc Baker," I said to Tilly.

As soon as the kitten was free, Tilly had trotted over to the bedroom door and begun scratching at it.

I crossed the room, knocked on the door, and called Pike's name. There was still no answer, but Tilly seemed frantic, so I slowly opened the door. "Pike?" I said as I set the kitten down and hurried inside the room. I bent down next to Pike's body to check for a pulse, but when I noticed the blood on the back of his shirt I knew he was dead.

I picked up the kitten, called to Tilly, and headed back to my Jeep. I called my brother, Mike, who told me to wait for him. The sky was almost completely dark by this point, so I turned on my headlights so I wouldn't feel quite so alone and isolated.

I knew I should call Bree to tell her I wasn't going to make it to book club despite my promise to do so, but she'd want a full explanation and ask a lot of questions, and I didn't think I was quite ready to talk about what I'd seen. Still, I didn't want her worrying about me, so I sent a quick text to let her know something had come up and I'd speak to her the following day.

When Mike arrived, he told me to stay put while he went inside. The kitten seemed to be in a playful mood despite his injured leg and Tilly appeared to adore him, so I let the antics of the animals distract me from what was going on inside. After twenty minutes or so, Mike came out of the cabin and approached the Jeep. He slid into the passenger seat and turned me toward him.

"Tell me exactly what occurred leading up to your finding Pike dead on his bedroom floor," Mike said.

"Tilly and I came by to drop off his mail. We were going to stop to chat for a bit. When Pike didn't answer the door, I figured he'd gone out, although I should have realized right away that he never went out when it was snowing."

"And after you arrived?" Mike encouraged.

"I knocked a couple more times and was going to leave, but Tilly wouldn't budge from the front porch. I wanted to check to make sure Pike was okay. I guess he wasn't."

"Did you see anyone else in the area?"

I shook my head. "It was already starting to get dark when we arrived, but I didn't see anyone. Pike's

Place opened at two. You can ask whoever's tending bar tonight if they saw or heard anything."

"I'll do that. It's been snowing all day. Did you notice footprints or tire tracks?"

"No. It was snowing hard when I got here. I'm sure any prints that might have been there have been covered by now. Who do you think did this?"

Mike frowned. "I wish I knew. Pike was shot in the back with a small-caliber weapon. I doubt he saw it coming." Mike glanced at the cabin, then back to me. "I noticed fishing supplies scattered across the floor."

"Pike was entering the old-timers' ice fishing competition with Hap this year. I guess he must have been going through his things before whoever killed him arrived. I think the kitten may be responsible for everything being on the floor."

"Okay. I'm going to be here for a while, so you may as well head home. I'll call you if I have any additional questions."

"Okay." I wiped away a tear that had slipped down my cheek. Pike was an old man I spoke to every couple of weeks and whose company I enjoyed, but I didn't know him well. Still, I knew his death would leave a hole in my life. "You need to catch whoever did this."

"Don't worry." Mike squeezed my hand. "I will."

I headed to Doc Baker's. I could probably fix up the kitten's leg with items I had in my cabin, but I wanted to make sure it didn't get infected. I pulled up in front of the veterinary clinic, parked in an empty space, picked up the kitten, and got out of my Jeep. The snow had gotten harder and the lights in the clinic were off, so I went to the front door of the house. Everyone knew if you had an animal emergency and it was after regular hours you could go to the front door and Doc Baker would take care of whatever you needed.

I knocked, and Tilly sat down next to me and waited. I could see lights coming on as someone made their way through the house. I cuddled the kitten to my chest while I waited for Doc Baker to come to the front of the huge house.

I was preparing myself with a smile and a greeting but froze the minute the door opened to reveal not a sixty-eight-year-old veterinarian in a white dress shirt but the most perfect man I'd ever seen wearing a towel around his neck and no shirt at all.

"You don't look like the pizza delivery guy." The man seemed as surprised to see me as I was to see him.

"And you don't look like Doc Baker." I couldn't help but stare at the absolutely gorgeous man wearing nothing but faded blue jeans.

He turned around, took a few steps inside, then returned to the door while pulling a T-shirt over his head of thick brown hair. "Sorry about that. I'd just gotten out of the shower when the pizza deliver guy called to let me know he was on his way." He looked at a point over my head. "In fact, there he is now."

"Is Doc Baker here?" I asked, uncertain how else to respond to this absurd situation.

"Doc Baker is my uncle and he's retired. I bought his practice. My name is Brady Baker. Why don't you come on in? I'll pay the pizza guy and then we can look at your kitten."

I hesitated, but I really wanted to have the kitten's leg looked at, and the Baker Veterinary Clinic was the only one in town. "Can Tilly come in as well?" I nodded toward the dog sitting next to me.

"Absolutely. If you head straight back, you'll see the door to the clinic on your left."

"I know where it is."

"Great. It's unlocked. Go ahead and wait for me there."

I fought the urge to flee as I slowly walked down the well-lit hallway. To be honest, I couldn't explain where the urge to abandon my mission and take the side exit out to my Jeep came from; maybe I'd simply been thrown for a loop when a gorgeous man close to my own age answered the door instead of the old friend I'd been expecting.

I entered the clinic and set the kitten on the exam table, then motioned for Tilly to sit down nearby. The kitten was favoring the injured leg but didn't appear to be in much pain, so I hoped the injury was minor and wouldn't require stitches or any other equally expensive procedure. I made decent money as a postal worker, but my Jeep was ancient and my cabin old and often in need of repair, and it seemed I was always having a hard time keeping up with the extra expenses. I leaned a hip against the table where I'd placed the kitten and gently played with him while we waited. After a few minutes, Dr. Hunk joined me, fully dressed in jeans, the T-shirt he'd slipped into at the door, and tennis shoes. His hands were free of pizza, so I assumed he'd dropped his dinner off in the kitchen before heading to the clinic. I felt bad he'd have to eat cold food but not bad enough to leave until I had the kitten's leg looked at.

"What do we have here, little fellow?" the man I couldn't seem to think of as Doc Baker asked.

"Meow."

Blue eyes met my brown eyes. "What's his name?"

"Name?" I asked.

"The kitten. What's his name?"

"Oh. I don't know. I just found him a little while ago. He was tangled up in fishing line. You can see he cut his leg. It doesn't look all that deep, but I wanted to be sure."

"It's always a good idea to err on the side of caution. I don't think he needs stitches."

"That's wonderful," I mumbled as I said a silent prayer of thanks.

"I'll clean him up and bandage the wound. It won't take long."

"Can I stay in here with him?" I asked.

"I don't see why not." He turned to collect the things he'd need. "I take it the dog is yours?"

"Tilly."

Tilly barked once when she heard her name. The new doc smiled, which caused a fluttering in my stomach I hadn't felt for a very long time.

"So, if this is Tilly, you must be Tess."

I frowned. "I am. How did you know?"

"I've heard all about you."

Great. "From who?" I had a feeling I already knew.

"From several people, actually, but most of my knowledge came from the pretty blonde who owns the bookstore."

"The pretty blonde is my soon-to-be ex-best friend, Bree. Please ignore everything she told you.

For some reason she feels it's her mission in life to fix me up with every even remotely eligible man who comes into town."

He chuckled. "I see. I guess that explains the rather long interview she conducted while she rang up my books." He handed me the kitten. "Here we go. He should be fine, but why don't you bring him back tomorrow for a quick look? He's a little on the young side to be away from his mama, so I'll give you some formula and bottles to supplement his food as well. You should be able to wean him off the formula in a couple of weeks."

"Okay. And thank you. I'm sorry I interrupted your dinner."

"It's not a problem."

"How much do I owe you?"

He paused. He lifted a dark, bushy brow that perfectly framed his bright blue eyes. "How about dinner?"

"You want me to buy you dinner?"

"No. I want you to share what's sure to be a cold pizza with me."

"Why?" I blurted out before I could consider my answer.

"Because I hate to eat alone and would enjoy the company."

I hesitated.

"It's just pizza. I promise."

"Okay," I agreed. "I guess I have time for a quick slice of cold pizza."

We returned to the house, and he led us to the kitchen, where a beautiful German shepherd was waiting.

"Tess, Tilly, meet Tracker."

Tilly walked over to the dog, who seemed to be waiting for some sort of a cue from the vet.

"At ease," he said, at which point Tracker began wagging his tail.

"At ease? Is the dog in the military?"

"No. But I used to be, so when I trained him, I used commands familiar to me. *At ease* means it's fine to chill because there isn't a job to do. Tracker was trained in search and rescue. I have a meeting next week with the local S and R team to see if they have a space for us."

"I'm sure they'll be thrilled to have you."

Tilly sniffed Tracker until she was satisfied he wasn't a threat, then was content to lay down on the rug in front of the brick fireplace, while Tracker settled onto a dog bed nearby. I set the kitten down beside Tilly because they seemed to have bonded and I didn't want him to be afraid of the new surroundings. Of course, the kitten decided it was time to play and not rest and immediately started running around the room, attacking every dust ball he could find.

"Sorry, I guess he's a bit wound up," I apologized.

"I'm glad to see the leg isn't slowing him down."

"He really is a whirlwind of energy," I agreed. "Which is probably how he got tangled in the fishing line in the first place." I chuckled as he jumped into the air and then did a complete three sixty before landing.

"I think you're going to have your hands full with this one. Wine?" he offered.

"I should stick to water. I still need to drive home and it's snowing pretty hard. I'll need to be alert."

He set a bottle of water in front of each of us, along with the pan of pizza he'd warmed momentarily in the oven.

"How long have you lived here?" I asked. "I wasn't even aware Doc Baker had retired."

"Just a couple of weeks. My uncle's been talking about retiring for quite some time, but he didn't want to leave until he was sure there was someone to take over the practice. At first I wasn't sure I wanted it, but after some soul-searching following a broken engagement, I decided maybe moving to White Eagle was a good idea after all."

"I'm sorry to hear about your breakup, but I'm happy to have someone take over the practice. Your uncle was the only vet in town."

"That was why he waited so long to retire."

I glanced at the kitten, who was now pouncing on Tilly's head. Being the patient dog she was, she just lay there and took whatever abuse the kitten dished out until he knocked a roll of gauze off the table and became hopelessly entangled once again.

"Looks like we have another tangle emergency." I laughed.

"Maybe that's what you should name him: Tangle," he suggested.

"I was thinking of something with a Christmas feel to it, like Mistletoe."

"Mistletoe is a good name now, but you may not feel the same when it's no longer Christmas. How about combining Tangle with Mistletoe?"

"Combining?"

"Tangletoe."

I laughed again. "That's a ridiculous name."

He grinned, looking me in the eye. "But you love it, right?"

I grinned back. "Actually, I kinda do."

Chapter 2

Tuesday, December 12

It had been a week since Pike's murder and so far, no one knew anything more than they had on the night I'd found him dead in his cabin. I did speak to Mike the day before, and he let on that he had a strong lead, which could, in fact, lead to a viable suspect, but for some reason he seemed less than thrilled about it. I almost had the feeling he hoped the lead wouldn't pan out, and that left me feeling a lot more worried than I liked to admit.

I'd never found the mama of the kitten, so I decided to keep him. He really was a cute little guy and Tilly seemed to adore him. As ridiculous as the new Doc Baker's suggestion of Tangletoe as a name had seemed, it appeared to have stuck, so I started calling him Tang. Tang needed to be fed every four hours at this point, so I fashioned a backpack for him and his supplies that Tilly carried so the kitten could go with us on our rounds. Once Tang got a little older I could leave him home, but for now, bringing him along seemed to be working out fine. He liked riding on Tilly's back and Tilly didn't seem to mind carrying him.

I'd just loaded my Jeep with the day's mail and was preparing to drive to the starting point of my route when I got an SOS from Bree. She wasn't the sort to make a mountain out of a molehill, so I took the message seriously and called her as soon as I settled Tilly and Tang in the Jeep.

"It's Tess; what's wrong?"

"Mike arrested Donny for Pike's murder."

Bree's news was so surprising I didn't respond immediately.

"Are you there?" Bree asked.

"I'm here," I answered. "I'm just trying to wrap my head around this. Why would Mike think Donny killed Pike?"

"I don't know." I could hear the panic in Bree's voice. "He said something about evidence and motive, but he didn't go into detail. You need to talk to Mike. Tell him that Donny would never kill anyone. You have to make him see there's no reason to lock the poor guy up."

I took a deep breath and let it out slowly. "Are you at the bookstore?"

"I'm here, but I haven't opened yet. I'm not sure I will."

"I'll go talk to Mike and then I'll come by."

I knew I'd need to hustle to catch up on my deliveries once I'd settled Bree down, but she was my best friend and I couldn't just leave her to deal with this crisis on her own. I stomped down the inkling that Donny might be guilty and focused on convincing Mike that he wasn't. When I'd first met Donny, he'd had a look I was drawn to and a certain childlike quality I'd found fun. After we'd dated for a while I'd realized his childlike quality often played out as childish irresponsibility, so when I realized Bree and Donny were attracted to each other, I was more than happy to step aside. Bree is a serious person most of the time, dedicated and hardworking, with little patience for slackers. I figured it would only be a matter of weeks before she realized Donny was a flake and dumped him herself, but they'd been together for almost six months, and if Bree didn't feel guilty that she had Donny and I had no one, I honestly think they'd be engaged by now.

"Mike in?" I asked his partner, Frank Hudson.

"In the back."

"He alone?"

Frank nodded.

"Can I leave Tang and Tilly out here with you?"

"I don't mind if they don't mind."

I took Tang out of the backpack and set him on the floor near Tilly and told Tilly to stay before I headed down the hall. Mike was alone in his office when I arrived at his door. He was looking intently at the computer screen and didn't see me until I spoke. "It looks like your lead paid off."

Mike looked at me, a frown on his face. "Afraid so. I'm sorry, Tess. I know you used to be sweet on Donny."

I walked the rest of the way into the office and sat down on the opposite side of the desk. "I'm not sweet on Donny. I'm not sure I ever was. But for some reason Bree is in love with the guy and I'm afraid she's having a total meltdown."

"Figured. She was pretty upset when she called earlier. I tried to explain to her why I had to arrest Donny, but she was so upset I don't think she was listening to what I tried to tell her."

"I'm not Brce and I'm listening. Why do you think Donny killed Pike?"

Mike hesitated before he answered. I'm sure he was weighing how much to share and how much to hold back, but I just needed something to tell Bree.

"Mike?"

He sighed and ran a hand through his thick brown hair before speaking. "It's just that this is an open investigation and therefore the details are sensitive, but I suppose Bree deserves to know what's going on." Mike leaned back in his chair, crossed his arms over his chest, and looked directly at me. I had a feeling he was watching me for my reaction. "After I spoke to you the night you found Pike's body, I went over to the bar, as you suggested, and spoke to Brick, the bartender. He said it had been quiet that afternoon, with the snow and all, but he'd seen Donny's truck in the parking lot earlier in the afternoon, though he never came in. I didn't think much of it at the time. I know Pike's visitors parked in the lot, but so did a lot of other people shopping in the area who didn't want to park on the street. Then, two days ago, I had an anonymous tip that Donny had been gambling and owed some very bad people a lot of money."

"Donny has been going to the casino? After what had happened before, I'd think the news would be all over town." Donny had a known gambling problem, and while there was a small casino in White Eagle, everyone knew it was in Donny's best interest to stay away from it. There were plenty of folks who would have called him out on his commitment to working on conquering his addiction.

"Donny has been going down to Missoula on his days off. There's a guy who runs an illegal high-stakes game in his warehouse. Anyway, from what I heard, he got in pretty deep with a moneylender out of Salt Lake who was threatening bodily harm if he didn't pay up."

I took a deep breath, then let the reality of the situation sink in. I slowly counted to ten before continuing the conversation. "Okay, so what does this have to do with Pike?"

"There's a rumor Pike had quite a lot of money hidden somewhere in his house."

"Why would he have money hidden in his home?"

"You know Pike. He was an old-timer set in his ways. He didn't trust banks to hold his social security checks. Why would he trust them with his life savings?"

Mike had a point. Everyone knew Pike came into the bank with his check every month and took the entire amount in cash rather than depositing it into a checking account.

"Okay, so you're operating under the assumption that Pike's money was real and somehow Donny found out about it, and he killed Pike to get to the cash so he could pay off the moneylender?"

"Exactly," Mike confirmed. "At first, I didn't want to believe it was true, but when I checked with my source, they said Donny's loan had been paid in full."

I had to admit that sounded pretty bad. Poor Bree; she was going to be crushed. "Did you ask Donny about the cash?"

"I did. He said he didn't know Pike all that well and had no idea he had any money in his cabin. I asked him how he managed to pay the moneylender and he said an old friend had given him a loan. When I asked for contact information for the 'old friend,' he said he was out of the country and unavailable."

"Sounds suspicious."

"I also found Donny's fingerprints inside Pike's house. I asked about them, and he said he stopped by to play cards now and then, but that was after he'd told me he didn't know the man all that well. I know this must be hard for Bree and I'm sorry about that, but I had to arrest him."

I found I agreed with Mike. It did look like Donny was guilty, and catching the bad guys and locking them up was what he was paid to do.

I left the police station, pulling the hood of my parka over my hair and heading down the snowy sidewalk with Tang and Tilly. I was going to be so late on my route I had no idea how I was going to catch up, but Bree was waiting for me at the bookstore. I wasn't sure what I was going to tell her; no matter how much I tried to soften the blow, she wasn't going to be happy. Based on what Mike had learned, though, it really did look as if Donny could be guilty.

I was so intent on my mission that I barely noticed the festive decorations provided by the town and vendors on Main. Not only did every light post have a bright green wreath wrapped up with a colorful red bow, but red and white lights were strung across the main thoroughfare, creating the feel of a magical Santa's village. When I arrived at the Book Boutique I noticed Bree had put a note on the door, letting everyone know the store wouldn't be open today due to a personal emergency. It occurred to me that she might have gone home, but her car was in the lot, so Tilly, Tang, and I went around to the back, where I figured the door to the alley could have been left open.

"Bree," I called as I entered the store.

"In the office."

I headed down the hallway to the small room where Bree did her paperwork.

"So?" she asked before I could even release Tang from the backpack.

I searched for the right words. It was obvious to me that Bree had been crying, but her perfectly applied makeup wasn't smudged in the least, so most people wouldn't notice. "I'm afraid Mike had a good reason to bring Donny in. It'll be up to the district attorney to decide whether to hold and charge him, but considering the evidence, I'd be surprised if he didn't."

"What evidence?" Bree demanded. "There's no way he did it."

I considered what to share and what to hold back. "Did you know Donny had been gambling?"

Bree didn't answer right away, but I could tell by the look on her face that she'd known about it. I waited for her reply rather than going on.

"I suspected he was gambling," Bree answered. "It seemed like he was going out of town a lot on his days off. He told me that his mom had been having some health problems, so he was going to Missoula to help her with some household chores, but when he started going almost every weekend I began to get suspicious. At first, I thought he had another girl on the side, but I confronted him and he told me that he loved me and would never do that. He assured me that he really had been staying with his mom, although he said he was also spending time with some of his old friends while he was there. I knew Donny'd had a gambling problem in the past, and when he started to be short of cash quite a lot I began to suspect. But even if that's true, what does it have to do with anything?"

"Donny's car was seen in the lot Pike shared with the bar. He didn't go into the bar, though Mike said it was possible Donny had just parked there to go to another shop in the area. The thing is, he found Donny's prints inside Pike's house."

Bree frowned but didn't respond.

"At first, Donny told Mike he barely knew Pike, but when Mike asked about the prints he changed his story and told him that he stopped by from time to time to play cards."

Bree looked at me with the strangest expression on her face. It was hard to know what she was thinking, but her bright blue eyes flashed with fear a split second before her expression changed to annoyance. "When is it a crime to either park in the lot behind the bar or play cards with an old man?"

"It's long been rumored Pike had a good deal of cash hidden in his house. According to Mike's source, Donny paid a gambling debt in full a couple of days after Pike was murdered."

Bree glared at me. "Do you actually think Donny killed Pike and stole his money?"

"Don't you?"

"Of course not. I know you were hurt when Donny dumped you for me, but to accuse him of something so awful is inexcusable. I thought you were my friend."

"I am your friend, and just for the record, I dumped Donny, not the other way around. But the fact of the matter is, Donny wasn't only seen near Pike's house on the day he died, he seemed to have motive to kill him."

"Tess Thomas, you're a mean, horrible person to say such a thing. Get out of my store this minute. I trusted you to help me get Donny free, but you're as misguided as your brother. If you won't help me, I'll prove Donny's innocence myself."

I wanted to argue, but I could see this wasn't the time, and I did have a mail route to get to, so I grabbed my dog and my kitten and headed to my Jeep without saying another word. I drove to the start of the route, slung my mail sack over my shoulder, and Tilly, Tang, and I started down the street at a brisk pace as we tried to make up the hour we'd just wasted attempting to help a friend who was either unable or unwilling to see the truth.

******

"You and Bree have been friends for too long to let this come between you," my mom said later that day when I stopped by to drop off her mail.

"I agree, but what am I supposed to do? Mike had a good reason to arrest Donny and Bree refuses to even consider he might be guilty."

"She's in love with the boy. Love can make you blind."

I grabbed a soda from the minifridge and popped the top. I'd let Bree's anger dig at me all day and now I felt like there was a volcano where my stomach should be. "I don't know what I can do at this point. Bree wanted me to talk Mike out of holding Donny, but the district attorney is involved now, so it's out of Mike's hands."

"I think Bree just wants to know you're on her side." Aunt Ruthie entered the conversation after she finished hanging a row of garland around the door. "She's your best friend, and that should mean something."

I let out a long groan. "It does mean something. You know how important Bree is to me. I tried to talk to her, but she wasn't listening to what I was trying to say."

"Donny is Bree's boyfriend. She's in love with him. She isn't going to let anyone tell her that her love has been misplaced. If she's going to come to that realization she's going to have to get there on her own. As her best friend, it isn't your job to convince her. You need to show her," Aunt Ruthie stated.

I picked up Tang, who had started to crawl up my leg. "Show her how?"

"She's your friend, so that's a question only you can answer," Mom counseled. "But if you want your relationship to survive, you'll need to find a way."

As Tilly, Tang, and I finished our route, I thought about Mom's words. I supposed she had a point. If it was the man I was in love with who'd been accused of wrongdoing, I'd probably be quick to take his side as well. The evidence Mike had was enough for an arrest, but it was far from conclusive. Maybe I should give Donny the benefit of the doubt until his guilt was either proven or disproven in a court of law. In the meantime, letting Bree know I was on her side and willing to work with her to prove Donny's innocence was probably the best move I could make.

******

"What are you doing here?" Bree asked when Tilly, Tang, and I showed up at her house that evening.

I held up a box from our favorite pizza joint. "I'm here to apologize."

Bree glared at me with a look of distrust.

"You were right this morning," I continued. "You asked me to help you and all I did was try to convince you that Donny was guilty. There are still a lot of things we don't know about Pike's death, so it's way too early in the game to put all our eggs in one basket. If you plan to prove Donny is innocent I'm here to help you do it."

Bree narrowed her gaze, as if she was trying to decide whether to believe me or not.

"Please," I begged, "you're my best friend and I love you. I hate it when we fight."

Bree smiled, her expression softening. "Okay." She stepped aside so the animals and I could come through the tile entry of her house. "I hate it too, and I need the help."

"Anything you need," I promised.

"Let's eat and we can discuss a strategy," Bree said.

I looked down at Tilly. "I'm sure her paws are wet."

Bree shrugged. "I'll grab her bed. If she gets mud on the carpet, I'll vacuum it up when you leave."

I waited until Bree fetched the large dog bed and then I settled both Tilly and Tang in for a nap. Bree and I were the closest of friends, but we had very different taste. Bree lived in a small house in town, just two blocks off the main thoroughfare, while I lived in a run-down cabin on a large lot outside town. Bree's house was of fairly new construction, furnished in a way that communicated a chic sophistication, while my cabin was decorated in a manner I thought of as rustic hodgepodge. Bree had cream-colored carpet, pale blue walls with white crown molding, a blue suede sofa with white pillows, and original art I knew had cost her a fortune, while I had a scuffed wood floor and a variety of tables and chairs I'd been given by friends or had found at the secondhand store.

"Do you know anything more now than what you told me this morning?" Bree asked as she worriedly nibbled on one of her perfectly manicured nails.

"No. I told you everything. Were you able to talk to Donny?"

"No. He's in holding until his arraignment. They don't allow visitors in holding. I checked to see if he was eligible for bail, but I was told that would be worked out in arraignment as well."

"And when will that be?"

"Friday."

I took a bite of the veggie pizza I'd brought because that was Bree's favorite. If Donny hadn't killed Pike—and in my mind that was still a huge *if*—

someone else had. All we needed to do was figure out who else had a motive for wanting the man dead. "Okay, this is what I think we need to do. We both speak to a lot of people during the average day. Everyone in town knew who Pike was. Some liked him, some didn't. It seems to me if we strike up conversations with the people we meet, someone is sure to say something that will point us in a direction. Was there someone with whom Pike had an altercation recently? Or could there be people who held a grudge against him? Longtime White Eagle residents like Hap would know if there'd been something brewing for a while."

"Okay," Bree said. "That sounds like a reasonable plan. Do you think you can get more out of Mike?"

"I think he's told me what he can for the time being. We'll do what we can to gather information tomorrow, then wait to see what happens on Friday. Maybe the judge will let Donny go and we can take a step back to let the police do their job."

"That would be best," Bree admitted. "Although I own a bookstore and love to read, especially mysteries, I've never once had the desire to investigate a real-life mystery."

"It could be interesting," I countered.

"Or dangerous."

"We might pick up some new skills."

"Or end up dead."

I paused and looked at Bree. "You do remember you're the one who wanted to do this in the first place."

"I know. And I do. I guess I'm just nervous. I mean, a man is dead and someone killed him. What if the real killer finds out we're trying to prove Donny is innocent? Wouldn't that make us a threat to whoever shot Pike in the back?"

Bree had a point. "For now, let's just engage people in conversation and see where that leads us."

"Do you think we should try to figure out whether Pike actually had any cash and, if he did, if it's missing?"

"I guess it wouldn't hurt to take a look around Pike's cabin. The door was open the last time I was there, although the police might have locked it. Though there's a small, ground-level window in the cellar that had a broken lock."

"How do you know the lock was broken?" Bree asked.

"Pike told me so when we spoke a while back. If it's still broken, we can probably get in that way."

"When should we go?" Bree asked.

I looked out the window. The most recent storm system had yet to arrive. "I'm thinking now. The bar is open, so the parking lot should be packed and our car won't stand out. And it's dark, so we can sneak around to the back if we need to."

Bree stood up. "Okay, let's do this."

"Do you want to change first?"

Bree was wearing a bright red sweater, a black wool skirt, and knee-high leather boots. "I'm fine. I'll grab my coat."

"Do you at least want to change your shoes?"

Bree looked down at the tip of one of her pointed toes. "I'm fine. These boots are plenty warm enough."

I shrugged. I seriously don't understand why anyone would wear high-heeled boots in the snow, but Bree always wore high heels and she seemed to manage okay. "We'll need a flashlight."

"I have a couple," Bree said. She paused and looked me in the eye. "Be honest: Do you think this is a good idea?"

I shrugged. "Probably not, but it's an idea and right now it's the only one we have. I want to stop by my place to drop off Tilly and Tang. You can ride along with me and I'll bring you back here when we're done."

******

I was right about the lot being jammed, but I found a place to park near the back, and Bree and I slid out of the Jeep and into the inkiness of the night. We first headed to the front door, but, as we suspected, it was locked, so we went around to the back and slipped in through the cellar window. Inside, it was completely dark, so we clicked on our flashlights. The cellar was below ground except for a row of small windows close to the ceiling, which was on the same level as a row of shrubs outside. They hid the windows, so I wasn't worried about someone nearby seeing our light.

It appeared Pike had used the cellar for storage. The walls were roughly finished, the floor a slab of cement. There were rows of shelves, the open kind, most stacked with emergency supplies such as canned goods, flashlights, flares, and blankets. I suppose having them made sense, especially for someone who'd been around as long as Pike. Even now, when a strong storm blew through town, there was a tendency for the electricity to go off and the roads to close.

"What are we looking for?" Bree asked as she ran a finger over a dusty surface, cringing slightly as she did so.

"I'm not sure," I admitted. "I can buy the fact that Pike had a bunch of cash and that he hid it in the house. We both know he didn't trust banks. Even if Donny's innocent, theft seems to me to be as good a motive as any."

"Of course, if that's true, and Pike did have cash his killer took, it won't be here to find," Bree pointed out.

"True. But we can look for a clue that indicates something that was recently here is now missing."

"Something like an empty drawer, slashed mattress or, better yet, an empty safe?"

"Exactly. We should also look for correspondence. Pike didn't get a lot of mail other than a few bills, but there could still be a clue in the items he did receive."

"Did Pike ever get mail of a personal nature? Maybe birthday or Christmas cards?" Bree asked.

"No. Never. At least until recently." I frowned. It suddenly occurred to me that the letter I'd delivered was most likely still lying on the floor just inside the front door. I made a mental note to look for it when we went upstairs.

"Do you remember if Pike received any bank statements? Just because he didn't put his money in the local bank doesn't mean he didn't have a savings account somewhere else." Bree began opening and closing the drawers in an old hutch that looked as if it hadn't been touched in years.

"Not offhand, but I'd be willing to bet he kept the mail he received stashed somewhere. He seemed to be the sort to hang on to things." I looked around the cluttered room. "I don't know how we're going to find anything in this mess."

"What about the boxes against the wall? There could be something important in one of them," Bree suggested.

"Let's look in them before we go upstairs."

As it turned out, most of the boxes held old clothes and household items, but we also found four large metal trunks. All had combination locks that had been cut. One of the trunks held photographs, one gold pans and picks from Pike's prospecting days, a third clothing and grooming items that would have belonged to a woman, and the last was empty.

"I wonder what was in this one," Bree said. We looked at each other, neither admitting we were thinking of the cash.

"I wonder who the woman's things belonged to," I said, diverting the conversation from the elephant in the room. I was going to need to call Mike to tell him about the trunk on the off chance he wasn't already aware of it, but I didn't want to have to reveal as much to Bree.

"Pike might have been married at one time," Bree suggested, "although I don't remember ever hearing about a wife being in the picture."

"He could be a widower. Pike must already have been in his sixties when we were born. If his wife passed before that, we wouldn't have had reason to know of her existence."

"I bet there are photos of her in that trunk."

"If Pike was married I'm sure there probably are photos of his wife, but we should stay on track. Though I'd love to have time to go through that trunk from top to bottom. Many of the photos look to have been taken of this area before White Eagle was even a town."

Bree picked up a photo that depicted five men standing in front of a mine entrance. "I bet the historical society would want these, unless, of course, Pike's next of kin comes to claim them."

I furrowed my brow. "I wonder who Pike's next of kin is." I glanced at Bree. "Do you ever remember him talking about a child or sibling?"

"No, never. Of course, if he ever was married his wife has been out of the picture for a long time, and he was ninety-two. If he had a child or sibling he'd most likely be pretty old himself." Bree stood up and looked around. "If the cash was in the empty trunk there's no way we can prove that now. The photos are interesting and could provide a clue to what happened to Pike, but my money is on the real clue being upstairs."

"I agree. Let's just hope the door between the cellar and the main part of the cabin is unlocked."

Luckily for us, it was.

The main part of the old cabin was exactly as I remembered it. There were dishes in the sink and coffee in the pot. A pair of old work boots stood by the front door, and a heavy jacket hung on a peg above that. The letter I'd delivered on the day I'd found Pike's body was still on the floor, although it had been shoved under a table. I bent down and picked it up, then slipped it into my jacket pocket before I closed the drapes so the light from our flashlights wouldn't be seen from outside. I wasn't sure where Pike would have kept important papers, but my bet was on the bedroom because there was no desk in the main living area.

The bedroom was at the back of the house, which lessened even further the likelihood that someone would see us from the parking area used by the bar. Bree began opening and closing drawers while I tried to pretend I wasn't imagining Pike on the floor at the foot of the bed. I was still having a hard time dealing with the fact that he was gone. In my mind, Pike and his stories of long ago were synonymous with White Eagle. He'd become something of a recluse in the past few years as his health declined, but when Tilly and I stopped by, he always had a treat for her and a story for me.

"Why don't you check the closet?" Bree said.

I realized I'd been standing in the middle of the room staring into space, and Bree's suggestion seemed to be as good as any. The closet, like many others, held clothes, shoes, and boxes stacked on a shelf. If there were any clues to be had, I figured they'd most likely be in one of the boxes, so I took them down and set them on the bed.

The first box, large and flat, held maps of the area. Old maps. The next held documents that looked like copies of land titles. I knew Pike had owned a lot of land in the area at one point, so perhaps when he'd gotten ready to sell it he'd needed to verify ownership. The titles could be a clue to why he'd been killed, so I set that box aside, beginning a pile I was going to take with me to investigate further.

The next box held old letters from someone named Patricia. They looked to be personal, so I set them aside. The boxes that looked like they'd originally held shoes now contained receipts. Hundreds, if not thousands, of receipts.

"Anything interesting?" Bree asked.

"The shoeboxes are filled with receipts. Most of them are from the gas station, grocery store, and pharmacist. I don't think there's anything relevant, but I suppose I should give them to Mike in case there's a clue in this mess."

Bree's face hardened. "I thought we were going to keep this investigation between ourselves."

"Mike's a cop and he's investigating this case. I said I'd help you, but I didn't agree to keep things from my brother. A man I cared about is dead. I know we're trying to prove someone other than Donny killed Pike, but in the end, isn't what we're really after the truth?"

Bree didn't respond, but I could see she didn't like the idea of helping Mike in the least.

Chapter 3

Wednesday, December 13

Tang, Tilly, and I got an early start on our route the following morning. I'd promised Bree I'd help her find out what really happened to Pike so Donny would be set free, but I had no idea where to start. I'd given the receipts to Mike, which, of course, initiated a whole slew of questions about where I'd gotten them. I'd tried to come up with a lame excuse about finding them in Pike's trash, which had blown over and I'd stopped to clean up. Naturally, Mike didn't believe a word I said, but at some point he'd realized arguing with me wasn't going to do any good because he allowed me to change the subject.

"Morning, Hattie," I said as I walked into Grandma Hattie's Bakeshop and was greeted with the wonderful smell of ginger and cinnamon.

"I have fresh cinnamon buns with cream cheese frosting if you're hungry."

"That sounds wonderful, but I'm in a bit of a hurry today."

Hattie crossed her arms and leaned forward on the counter. "Why is it you young folks are always in such a hurry? Life should be savored and enjoyed, not rushed through from one minute to the next like you're in some sort of race to the finish line. Trust me, when you get to be my age you're gonna wish you'd taken the scenic route."

I set Hattie's mail on the counter. "I know you're right. And most days I do try to slow down and enjoy the moments of my life. But I promised Bree I'd help her look in to Pike's death, so I'm hoping to finish my route early."

"Bree is investigating Pike's death? Why on earth would she be doing something like that?"

"It's not that she's so keen on investigating; she wants to find some sort of proof that Donny didn't do it."

"I heard Mike arrested Donny." Hattie cut a cinnamon roll in half, keeping one half for herself and sliding the other to me. I wanted to remind her that I didn't have time to eat, but with all that melted frosting it sure did look good, so I broke off a corner and popped it into my mouth. "There's something different about this frosting. Did you add something new?"

"Amaretto. Just a splash, but it adds a unique flavor."

This was without a doubt one of the best cinnamon rolls I'd ever had. "This really is delicious, but I should be going. Do you want me to deliver muffins to Hap?"

"No. I took some by the store myself this morning because I needed to stop by to confirm the details for our date night."

I took another bite of the roll before wiping my fingers on a napkin. "Has it occurred to you that separating from a man you obviously care for after forty years of marriage only to continue to date him is insane?"

"Is it?" Hattie asked. "When we were married Hap took me for granted. Even though I worked all day, same as him, he expected that when we got home in the evening I'd make the meals and clean the house. Now that he has his own home he does his own cooking, cleaning, and laundry, and when we're together, he treats me with the kindness and respect he didn't always bring to our marriage."

I supposed that made sense in a twisted way. It was obvious neither Hap nor Hattie were dating anyone else and they seemed to be happy with their lives. I wasn't sure the arrangement would work for me, but who knew how I'd feel after forty years of marriage to the same guy.

"I guess I see what you mean, but it must get lonely at times."

"At times," Hattie agreed.

"Thanks for the roll and the conversation, but I should get going if I want to have time to help Bree as promised." I lifted my bag back onto my shoulder.

"Are you sure you want to get in the middle of things?" Hattie asked again.

"Want to, no. But I promised."

"Things might not turn out the way you hope," Hattie continued. "I heard Donny's been gambling again."

"I heard that as well, but Bree is sure he didn't kill Pike and she's my best friend. She asked me to help, so I'm going to."

"In that case, I might know something interesting that will help."

"Okay." I set my bag back down. "What do you know?"

"I was over at the bar delivering some sweet bread to Brick yesterday. Apricot oatmeal, to be exact. It's his favorite, you know. Anyway, I was just leaving the bar when I saw a car pull into the parking area. It looked to be a rental, so I took a minute to watch. A nicely dressed gentleman who looked to be in his midsixties got out of the sedan and walked up to Pike's door. He knocked and waited, and I did the neighborly thing and went over to let him know Pike had passed on. The man, whose name, I learned, was Andrew Barton, seemed to be both surprised and dismayed. I invited him back to the bakery for a cup of coffee; it was a slow time of day, so I poured myself a cup and sit to chat with him for a bit."

"And...?" I hoped Hattie would speed things up a bit.

"Andrew told me that he'd come to White Eagle to meet Pike. Apparently, he's a retired college professor who's writing a book about the history of this part of Montana and he'd been corresponding with Pike via email for quite some time. He told me that while Pike was a well of information, he was unwilling to share anything really juicy about this town or the colorful individuals who'd lived here during his lifetime. Andrew tried to prod some small-town gossip out of Pike, but he said he seemed uneasy about sharing secrets with someone he'd never met in person. Andrew didn't know for certain Pike would give him any dirt even if he showed up to meet him, but he thought it might be worth the effort to try. He emailed to let him know he was coming, then made travel arrangements."

"Did he have any idea what sort of secrets Pike might be keeping?"

"Andrew had no idea. Pike was very careful to say just enough to pique his interest but not enough to give him the context of any secrets he was guardian to."

"Is the man still in town?"

Hattie shrugged. "Don't know. I do know that when he left here he was heading to the inn."

I thanked Hattie for the information and continued on my route.

If Pike was involved in an email exchange with a man who was interested enough in hearing what he had to say to travel here in December, I figured those emails might lead us to a clue. Of course, the very existence of a clue left me feeling conflicted. Bree would have a fit if I brought Mike in on the information I'd just learned, and Mike would have a fit if I didn't. The inn wasn't on my route, but I decided to stop by to see if Mr. Barton was still in town, and if he was, if he'd be willing to speak to me.

******

The Inn at White Eagle is a warm, cozy lodging built from hand-milled logs from trees grown nearby.

It's situated on the edge of one of the smaller lakes in the area that isn't deep enough for motorboats but is perfect for lazy days spent fishing or simply sitting on the front porch contemplating the universe.

"Afternoon, Tess. What are you doing all the way out here?" the innkeeper, Megan Rosenberg, asked.

"I'd like to speak to Andrew Barton if he's available. Hattie gave me his name."

Megan leaned on the counter in front of her. "He did have a reservation but ended up staying for only one night. It seems he was here to see Pike and when he learned he'd passed on he decided to cancel the rest of his reservation. Shame; he was such a nice man. I would have enjoyed getting to know him better."

"I don't suppose you have his contact information?"

"I do, but I'm not at liberty to give it out. Why did you want to speak to him?"

I took a piece of peppermint candy from the jar on the counter and popped it into my mouth. "Hattie told me that he was in town to speak to Pike about a secret he'd been keeping. I know it's a long shot, but I hoped Mr. Barton might have information that could provide a clue as to why he was murdered."

"You think some secret Pike was keeping led to his death?"

I shrugged. "I don't know, but at this point I'm following every lead that comes my way."

"I heard Donny Dunlap was arrested for Pike's murder. I figured the case was closed."

"Donny was arrested," I confirmed. "Bree is sure he's innocent, so I agreed to help her find the truth."

Megan walked out from behind the counter and headed into the main common area, where a giant tree brightened the room with colorful lights. Near the tree was a secretary's desk that I thought must be used as a communication center. She opened a drawer and took out a paper, then walked back across the room and handed it to me. "Have you met Wilma Cosgrove, the new librarian?"

"No, not yet."

"This is her cell number. She wanted to speak to Mr. Barton too. She'd heard he was in town to speak to Pike and hoped to catch him before he left. When I informed her that he'd already left she asked if I'd pass her number along if I spoke to him. It seems she has information about Pike that she thought he would be interested in. The library's open for another forty minutes. If you hurry you can catch her."

I hugged Megan. "Thanks, Meg. I'll head over there now."

I felt bad telling Tilly that she was going to have to wait in the Jeep again, but dogs weren't allowed in the library and I'd only be a few minutes. Besides, she had Tang to entertain her. They'd be fine until I returned. The new librarian had moved to White Eagle less than a month ago and I'd heard she was a nice woman the locals thought was going to fit right in. Unlike the previous librarian, who'd lived here since before I was born and had recently retired at the age of sixty-five, Wilma was fresh out of college.

"Can I help you?" Wilma asked as I approached the front counter.

I smiled. "I hope so. We haven't met yet, but my name is Tess Thomas."

"Of course." Wilma's bright green eyes sparkled with delight. "I've heard so much about you and your dog. I hoped you'd stop in so we could get to know each other. I have a golden retriever and thought it would be fun to set up a doggy playdate."

Okay, common ground. That was good. Maybe she'd be more apt to share with me what she knew. "I'm sure Tilly would love that. What's your dog's name?"

"Sasha. She just turned one and has a lot of puppy enthusiasm, so I really appreciate dog owners who are willing to allow their canine buddies to help her work off some of her excess energy."

"I'll give you my number and we can arrange a time."

"That would be great."

I jotted down my number and handed it to the perky young woman.

"So, how can I help you today?" Wilma asked.

"I heard you had some information about Pike Porter. I'm not sure if you've heard, but Pike and I were friends and I'm looking in to his death in an unofficial way."

Wilma's face grew serious. "I heard you were the one who found his body. That must have been devastating for you."

"It was. I've known Pike most of my life. I won't say we were best friends, but he lived on my route and I stopped in to visit with him as often as I could. Of course the police are investigating, but I'm finding it difficult to sit by and do nothing."

"You don't think the man they're holding is guilty?"

I hesitated for just a moment before answering. "To be honest, I'm not sure whether Donny Dunlap is guilty, but I don't think I'll be able to let go of this until I'm sure."

Wilma waved a finger, indicating I should follow her. She led me into a back room and closed the door. "I totally understand how you feel, and I'll help you if I can. I don't know if the information I have is important, but I feel as if it might be. I spoke to the cute cop investigating the case, but I could tell by the look on his face that he didn't think what I told him was particularly valuable."

I figured either Wilma had spoken to Hank or, if she'd spoken with Mike, she hadn't put together Mike's last name and my own. I decided to leave a discussion of the interrelatedness of the town's residents for another time.

At any rate, Wilma continued before I had a chance to respond. "During the week before his death, Pike came into the library twice. Both times he wanted to look at old newspapers that have been kept in the archives in the back ever since they were donated by the last owner of the newspaper when he retired and left White Eagle. Pike never said what he was looking for, but he requested articles from the very first newspapers circulated back in the nineteen forties."

That was interesting, but Pike was an old man and he could have just wanted to take a stroll down memory lane. "Did you notice if he seemed interested in anything in particular?"

Wilma shook her head of short blond curls. "As I said, he didn't say what he was after, but I noticed he turned to the back of the paper, where births and deaths, land transfers, mining claims, and other information that didn't warrant an entire article were listed."

I wasn't sure what I could do with this piece of information, though it did seem Pike had been looking for something specific. Might he have found it and might that have been what had gotten him killed?

"I appreciate you sharing this with me. I know you're about to close; I may come back to look at the old newspapers myself sometime if that's okay."

"That's fine. Anytime. And I'll call about a doggy playdate."

"Maybe this weekend?"

"That would be perfect."

I pondered my options as Tilly and Tang settled into the Jeep for the ride home. I felt like I had a lot of clues that felt significant, but I wasn't sure how they fit together. After contemplating the situation for several minutes, I decided on the only thing that seemed to make sense. I needed to find out what was in the emails between Pike and Andrew Barton Hattie had referred to, and for that I'd need to call on an old friend and the only person on earth who knew *my* secret: Tony Marconi.

******

I first met Tony when he transferred into my school during the seventh grade. Tony was a genius of sorts who probably should have been enrolled in some sort of school for gifted students, but his mother wanted him to have a normal life, and for some reason, in her mind, the tiny school in White Eagle met her definition of normalcy. When I first met him, I thought he was the biggest dork to ever walk the face of the earth. Sadly, like the other kids in my class, I was less than kind to him in the beginning. Not only was he smarter than everyone else in the entire school, including the high school students and most of the teachers, he was the tallest kid in the school as well. In a nutshell, when the goal of every seventh grader is to fit in and be part of the crowd, Tony stood out like a giraffe in a herd of zebras.

I guess the turning point in our relationship occurred when I was fifteen. I was nosing around in the attic of the house Mike and I lived in with our mother and found a letter hidden in a book I believed to be encrypted—yes, I devoured mysteries like my life depended on it, and, yes, in those days I thought every old letter I found must be encrypted. This letter had been stashed in a book that had been stored with some items my dad had tucked away in the attic before he died in a fiery truck accident while driving the cross-country route he had been working most of my life. Believing it could somehow provide an answer to the questions I'd been dealing with since his death, I decided to try to break the code. After dozens of failed attempts, I realized I had no choice but to enlist Tony's help. As it turned out, the letter hadn't been encrypted at all, but our search had led us to uncover some anomalies in my father's death, which is what I had suspected all along. We decided to keep our search to ourselves as we continued to dig, and in the end, the time I spent with Tony trying to find answers that ultimately weren't there had cemented a friendship that has endured to this day.

Once I decided to enlist Tony's help, I drove to Pike's cabin and snuck back in through the cellar. I knew taking his laptop probably crossed some sort of line that could land me in jail next to Donny, but after mulling things over, I'd come to feel reading the emails between Pike and Andrew Barton was the most urgent thing I needed to do. Tony lived in a mansion on a private lake about twenty miles out of town, so I called ahead to make sure he was home. He not only was there but he was thrilled to hear from me, so I fed Tang and Tilly, then loaded them into the Jeep and headed north up the mountain.

As I drove up the narrow, winding road, I thought about the unique relationship Tony and I shared. Other than Bree, I considered Tony to be my best friend. Not only did we share a secret, but we also shared a love of gaming that gave me a reason to drive out to his place a couple of times a month to battle zombies and save the world from the domination of evil. Being a well-known tech head, Tony had access to games that weren't on the market yet, and he was the only person in my life who could beat me on a regular basis. I love a challenge, and when it came to gaming Tony provided just that.

I turned on my brights as I pulled off the highway and onto the narrow road leading to Tony's home. I'm not sure why he chose to live in isolation. As an absolute genius, he had the potential to live in a penthouse, drive imported cars, and date beautiful women while making billions in the world of technology, yet he chose to live in seclusion miles away from the nearest town. Don't get me wrong: Tony isn't wasting his talents. I'm not sure exactly who he works for or what he does, though I do know that while he seems to spend his days locked away alone, he's amassed a fortune he seems to have earned developing software for the FBI, CIA, NSA, or some other equally secret-worthy institution. I've tried a time or two to pry the details of what he does out of him, but he just smiles and tells me I'm cute when I'm frustrated.

Tony was chopping wood for his fireplace when Tilly, Tang, and I arrived. Tilly bolted out of the car as soon as I opened the door, which left Tang hissing in a hunchbacked position at the unanticipated disappearance of his best friend. Tilly loves Tony. I mean really loves him. Every time we come for a visit Tilly forgets her training and leaps out of the car in a bullet race to him before I can even get the door all the way open.

"Don't worry," I said to Tang as I picked him up and cuddled him to my chest. "Tilly still loves us. She just hasn't seen Tony for a while and she misses him."

I couldn't help but smile as Tilly leaped onto Tony's chest, almost knocking him to the ground while she showered him with wet doggy kisses.

When Tony and Tilly had finished greeting each other they headed to me and Tang, waiting near the Jeep.

"Who's this?" Tony asked, reaching for Tang, who hissed at him.

"This is Tilly's new kitten, Tangletoe, Tang for short."

"Tangletoe?" Tony asked.

"A name the cute new veterinarian in town came up with, combining tangle with mistletoe. It's a long story. I'll fill you in later."

"Cute new veterinarian?"

"Dr. Baker retired and his nephew took over. It's freezing out here. I'll grab the laptop and we can continue this conversation inside."

Once Tony got the laptop in his hands he was all business. He headed to the cellar, where he kept his computer equipment. The room had no windows and a single doorway he kept locked when he wasn't inside. I'd often thought that, although the sub-ground-level room seemed to be secure, it wouldn't be a good place to be trapped in a fire. To be honest, I was usually uncomfortable in the room, with equipment I was sure was probably worth millions of dollars, but I set aside my uneasiness and watched as Tony dusted off the laptop and set it down on a spotlessly clean table at the back of the spotlessly clean room. When he had the laptop where he wanted it he hooked it up to his own system, or at least a portion of it, and began working. He saw right away that Pike had password-protected his computer, but he assured me that wouldn't keep him out for long.

"There's chili on the stove," Tony commented as his fingers flew over the keyboard so fast I could barely see them.

"Homemade?"

"Homemade is the only kind of chili I eat. It's simmering on the back burner."

"I'm hungry and I do love your chili. Can I bring you some?"

"No, thanks. I had a late lunch, so I'll eat when I finish with your project."

I headed upstairs, were Tang and Tilly were waiting. Tilly knew she wasn't allowed in the computer room, but Tony had set up a dog bed filled with toys near the fireplace, so she never seemed to mind being left alone here for short periods of time. Most of the time when I came over it was to watch television or to play video games, which we did in the main living area where all Tony's guests, including the four-legged, furry kind, were allowed.

As I made my way through the clean but somewhat cluttered first floor, I marveled at the view of the lake just beyond the wall of windows that made the open living area feel like you were outside among the trees. I loved sitting on Tony's sofa and looking at the lake, but tonight I felt antsy, so I flipped on the television and continued to the kitchen.

I scooped a large portion of chili into a brown ceramic bowl, grabbed a beer from the refrigerator, and returned to the main living area. I clicked around the channels, finally settling on the Hallmark Channel, which was showing a Christmas movie that was just touching enough to maintain my interest. Tilly curled up on the sofa next to me and Tang curled up in the space between Tilly's front paws and head. I'm not sure at what point I fell asleep, but the next thing I knew the movie was over and Tony was standing in front of me with Pike's laptop in his hands.

"Sorry. I must have dozed off. Did you get in?"

"Of course. Let me grab a beer and a bowl of chili and I'll fill you in."

Another Christmas romance had come on while I was sleeping, which I figured Tony wouldn't want to watch, so I turned off the television and gathered my empty bowl and beer bottle to take to the kitchen, where he was putting away the leftovers. We both returned to the living area and I listened while he ate and told me what he'd found.

"The emails from Pike to Andrew Barton mostly describe the history of the area. Pike did a good job of painting a picture of the trappers who first settled here, following the miners who hoped to strike it rich but mainly died in poverty and, even later, the lumber barons, headed by Hank Weston and Dillinger Wade, who realized the trees growing in the dense forest were the real gold."

I knew Hank Weston had met Dillinger Wade at the mining camp. Dillinger had family money and Hank struck it rich in mining, and the two men joined forces and built an even larger fortune in the lumber industry. They eventually founded the town of White Eagle in 1945. Hank met Dillinger's sister, Hillary, when she came to visit and the two married and had three sons who now owned a good portion of the land in the area.

"Pike provided other historical facts, followed by colorful accounts of some of the people he'd met as the town grew and developed," Tony continued. "Pike was born to one of the miners in 1925, so by the time Weston and Wade began developing the town he was already a young man living on his own and operating the bar. While I found the emails interesting, I didn't find anything relevant in terms of honing on a motive for his murder. In the final three or four emails Pike did hint at a secret he'd kept for most of his life that had weighed heavily on him in his later years. Barton, of course, was all over that, encouraging him to share what he knew, but Pike insisted the consequences could be far-reaching even today and wasn't sure he wanted to trust what he knew to someone he'd never met."

"Which is why Andrew Barton was in town."

"It would seem."

Tony finished his chili and took his bowl into the kitchen. I followed.

"There must be something else on the computer that might give us a hint about the secret Pike referred to."

"There are a lot of files on the computer. I didn't take the time to look at all of them, but one of them was called 'Bloomfield Mine.' I opened it and found copies of old maps that look to me to be claims of mines that go back to the early twentieth century. I saw the shaft Weston struck it rich mining was right next to a claim that belonged to Bloomfield, whoever he was. I'm not sure if that's significant, but it could be worth looking in to."

"I found maps and land titles in boxes in Pike's cabin. I took a couple of them home, but I haven't had a chance to go through them yet. And the new librarian told me that Pike had come in a couple times in the week before his death to look at old newspapers from the nineteen forties."

"It seems Pike knew or wanted to prove something that had been gnawing at him for a whole lot of years. I wonder if he found what he was looking for."

I poured myself a cup of coffee that had most likely been sitting on the heating plate all day, then leaned against the counter while Tony rinsed the dishes and stacked them in the dishwasher. "I wish I knew. I feel like we're on to something, but I still have no idea how any of this ties in to Pike's death."

"If you want to leave the computer I'll dig around some more tomorrow."

"Okay; thanks." I reached my arms over my head in a deep yawn. "I guess I should gather up the kids and get going. If you find anything interesting call or text me."

"Are you sure you're okay to drive?"

"I'm sure." I stood on tiptoe and kissed Tony on the cheek. "And thanks again for everything." I walked into the living room and began gathering the dog and cat.

"If you want to drop off the maps and other materials you found tomorrow I'd be willing to look at them as well. Maybe we can find some kind of pattern."

"I'll call you tomorrow afternoon. This week has been crazy busy; I need to figure out what I still need to accomplish before the weekend." I looked around the room. "You don't have a tree."

"A tree?"

"A Christmas tree. You don't have one."

Tony looked momentarily confused. "No, I don't have a tree. I've never had a tree, and in all the years I've known you, you've never once pointed that out."

I cuddled Tang to my chest. "I guess it just hit me how really un-Christmassy this place is. If you want I can come by this weekend to help you find a tree."

Tony smiled. "I'd like that."

"You'll need lights and a few ornaments. I'll try to pick some up."

Chapter 4

Thursday, December 14

By the time Tang, Tilly, and I had gotten home last night it was practically time to get up. To say I was dragging a bit as I showered, dressed, and drank my first two cups of coffee was an understatement. As I downed my third cup, I was beginning to feel a bit more human. I'd spent a lot of time thinking about Pike and the files on his computer. I wasn't sure exactly what the emails and files were leading to, but I felt like we could very well be on to something that could prove Donny hadn't killed Pike. I knew I should turn Pike's computer over to Mike, but I wanted to give Tony time to find the secret Pike had been hiding, so I'd simply avoid Mike for a few days. When I finally ran into him, I could fill him in without having to lie or leave out any details.

"Morning, Pete," I said as I entered Pete's Pets with a stack of mail. Tilly loved to look around at all the various animals, but she'd been trained to stay right next to me so she didn't scare the fish, rabbits, and other small animals Pete sold. "Looks like your invitation came through for the mayor's gala." I reached into the pack and picked up Tang. I wasn't sure he could get out of the pack on his own, but the last thing I needed was him trying to attack the parrot that was sitting on a perch behind the counter.

"To be honest, I sort of hoped the mayor would overlook me this year," Pete grumbled. "I know it's an honor to be invited, but the gala is always on a Thursday and I have poker with the guys on Thursdays."

"So don't go." I tossed the pile of mail with the invitation on top onto the counter.

"I wish it was that easy. The wife considers it our duty as members of one of the two founding families to attend. I don't suppose you could pretend the invitation got lost and you never delivered it to me?"

I shook my head. "Sorry. It's my job to make sure all the mail I'm entrusted with is delivered in an efficient and timely manner."

"Figured. Guess I should have considered the consequences of marrying Hank Weston's granddaughter when I proposed to Doris."

I suppressed a chuckle at Pete's posturing. He was doing a good job making it seem as if he was the wounded party, but everyone knew it was Doris's money that had paid for not only the pet store but the big house the couple shared with their three children.

"I know the gala is probably boring to you, but I think it's nice that the descendants of the Westons and Wades still get together once a year to raise money for the community. Marrying Doris did come with an obligation, but it also came with a privilege.

Besides, I happen to know both Austin Wade and Adam Weston will be at the gala, both of whom are part of your poker group, so I'm sure the game will be postponed."

Pete sighed. "I suppose you have a point."

"By the way, while we're on the subject of our founding fathers, I was curious whether you had any documents or photos dating back to the time White Eagle was founded."

Pete shook his head while he thumbed through the mail I'd just delivered. "My family isn't from the area and Doris's parents have all the records and photographs passed down through her family. Why do you ask?"

"I was just curious. There was a historian in town who seemed to have a lead to some huge secret that dated back to that time and I was curious."

"I don't know about a secret, but I wouldn't be surprised. The men who put down roots and established the town were rich and powerful. In my experience, rich and powerful men become that way because they're willing to do whatever it takes to get what they want. I'm sure there are a few skeletons in the closets of both our founding fathers."

Pete was probably right. It made sense there was more than one secret waiting to be uncovered, but I was starting to seriously believe there was one that had gotten Pike killed. I decided to spend my lunch hour trying to figure out what Pike had been looking for in the library. Tang and Tilly wouldn't be allowed inside, so I dropped them off in my cabin first. After greeting Wilma and spending a few minutes in idle chitchat, she showed me to a table where I could look at the newspapers. She'd told me Pike had been interested in the back of the newspaper, where birth and death announcements, among other notices, were printed. I wasn't sure where to begin my search, so I started scanning each paper, hoping something popped out. Eventually, I found a notice that had been circled in pencil: the announcement of the birth of Austin Wade, the oldest of the three children born to Dillinger Wade and his wife Alberta. I couldn't be certain Pike had been the one to circle it, or even if it was relevant to his murder if he had, but I took down the information just in case.

******

I'd just finished my route and was heading back to the Book Boutique to give Bree a report on what Tony and I had learned when I ran into the handsome new veterinarian coming out of the shop. Tilly seemed to remember him; she trotted right over to say hi. After greeting Tilly, Dr. Baker removed Tang from the pack and cuddled him to his chest.

"Seems like our patient healed up just fine," he said as Tang pawed his face.

"You'd never know he had an injury," I answered. "He may be small, but he's a tough little thing. Thanks again for fixing him up."

"No problem. It is, after all, my job."

"That's true, but you were very nice, considering we interrupted your dinner. I heard you're planning a pet adoption clinic at the shelter this weekend. If you need help I'll be happy to volunteer for a few hours. I've helped out at the clinics your uncle held in the past."

"That would be great. I scheduled the clinic before I found out the orientation for search-and-rescue volunteers was this weekend. I really want to attend so I can get started, but we have a full house, so I didn't want to cancel the clinic."

"I'd be happy to fill in for you. I'm sure the S-and-R team will benefit from your participation, so it seems important for you to get started."

"I'll be away the entire morning."

"Don't worry; I'll take care of everything. Do you have flyers?"

"I have a stack in my car I haven't gotten around to passing out."

"I'll take a handful and distribute them while I'm doing my rounds tomorrow. I think you'll be surprised by how much support you'll get. There may not be enough families in the market to adopt a dog right now to place all the animals, but I bet you'll be able to place a few and recruit some volunteers while you're at it."

"With everything I've taken on, volunteers would be great."

I smiled. "Leave it to me. I'll call you tomorrow to finalize the details."

"Better yet, how about dinner? My treat, as a thank-you for helping me out of a bind."

"Okay," I said. "Text me the time and place and I'll meet you."

Brady and I chatted about restaurant options as I followed him back to his car. He handed me the stack of flyers and I promised to make sure they found their way onto all the bulletin boards in town provided for announcements and local events. Having a haven for the strays in town was a cause that was near and dear to my heart, and if I had to put in a few extra hours making sure everyone knew about the clinic, putting in a few extra hours was fine with me.

After we said our good-byes to Brady, Tang, Tilly, and I headed back to the bookstore. The shop was closed, but Bree was still there cleaning up, so when she saw us at the front door she unlocked it and invited us in.

"I thought you were going to be here by six," she said after I'd taken off my coat and released Tang from my backpack.

"I *was* here at six, but I ran into Brady Baker as he was leaving and we stopped to chat for a few minutes."

Bree smiled. "You like him."

I shrugged. "Of course I like him. He's a very nice man."

"Not to mention drop-dead gorgeous."

I actually blushed. "I guess he is rather good-looking." I paused as I spotted the gleam in Bree's eyes. "But that doesn't mean I'm looking for anything more than friendship, so don't start planning our wedding. Dr. Baker is just a nice man with whom I have common interests. I plan to help with his adoption clinic."

Bree tried to look innocent and nonchalant as she shelved books that had been left in the reading area, but I knew she was plotting ways to get Brady and me into a relationship. Matchmaking seemed to be in Bree's blood. No matter how many times I'd told her to stay out of my love life, it seemed every time I turned around there she was, meddling where she ought not be.

"He mentioned the clinic," Bree commented. "I'm glad you're volunteering again. It's a good cause and I know you enjoy it."

"I do, and I'm glad I ran into him, but the real reason I'm here is to catch you up on what I've discovered about Pike."

Bree stopped what she was doing and turned to look at me. "You found something?"

"Maybe." I leaned a hip against the counter. "I found out a man named Andrew Barton was in town to meet with Pike about some sort of secret he had but wouldn't share via email. Pike died before they could meet, so Barton left. Still, if Pike knew something with wide-range implications, it occurred to me there may be someone who had an interest in making sure he never had the opportunity to tell anyone what he knew."

Bree grinned. "If Pike was killed because of something he knew, Donny must be innocent."

"That's my current theory. Of course, we need to prove it."

"How?"

"It seems to me the first step is to figure out what it was Pike was thinking of sharing with Barton."

Bree looked confused. "How will we do that?"

"Tony has Pike's computer and is working on it. In fact, I'm going to his place as soon as I change. When I left Tony's last night he'd managed to gain access to his files, but he hadn't had a chance to really look around. I'm hoping by now he has news for me. I also said I'd drop off the boxes we found with the maps and deeds. Tony's the smartest person I've ever met. If there's something to find he'll find it."

Bree reached out to hug me. "Thank you. When you first said you were going to help me find Pike's real killer so Donny would be released, I wasn't sure your heart was in it, but I can see now you took things seriously and have been working on it."

"Of course. You're my best friend."

"How can I help?" Bree asked.

"I guess you could come with me over to Tony's."

Bree scrunched up her nose. I knew she still saw him as the nerd we both at one point believed him to be. "I had a late night last night and would love to have some company on the drive up and back," I added.

"Oh, okay. I need to go home, though, and put on clothes I don't mind getting dusty. Do you want to pick me up in a half hour?"

"Make it forty-five minutes. I need to go home and change, load the boxes with the maps and deeds into the Jeep, and then pick up some Chinese takeout. I'll swing by to get you after that."

Bree agreed, although she still looked less than thrilled. "I'll be ready."

******

In retrospect, I think things would have been fine if Tony's friend Shaggy, who liked to tease Bree about everything, hadn't visited on the same night Bree and I did. Shaggy, whose real name was Stuart, was tall and lanky, with longish blond hair. He owned a small computer store in town that mainly did repairs and sold video systems and video games. New computers could be ordered through his shop, but most folks either ordered their own hardware online or waited until they planned to travel to one of the larger cities with a wider selection.

"You didn't tell me Mr. Annoying was going to be here," Bree complained when we pulled up and saw Shaggy's van."

"I didn't know or I would have warned you. I know you don't like him, but he's pretty harmless. If he teases you just ignore him."

"Easy for you to say; he never hassles you."

"He doesn't hassle me because I ignore him. You're too easily baited, which makes hassling you all kinds of fun." I reached over and grabbed Tang. I didn't want to take the chance that he would jump out of the Jeep and become lost in the dark. Tilly hopped down on her own after Bree and I got out. Bree picked up the Chinese takeout and I got Tang and Tilly's dinner before we went to the front door.

"Well, if it isn't Tess and her carry-on," Shaggy said when he answered the door.

I could almost hear Bree growl, but she didn't say anything as she pushed past Tony's somewhat colorful friend and headed toward the kitchen.

"You might want to lay off the short jokes," I whispered to Shaggy as Bree went down the hallway.

Shaggy grinned. "Why? It's fun to tease her. She gets so ruffled."

"Bree might look like a tiny porcelain doll, but she has a temper. If you're as smart as you think you are you might not want to get her too riled up."

Shaggy saluted. "Yes, Mom."

I rolled my eyes but didn't engage with the man-child who seemed to think he was charming when he clearly wasn't. "I'm going to let Tony know we're here. I'll only be a minute. Play nice while I'm gone."

I settled Tang and Tilly into the large dog bed, then headed down the stairs to the cellar. If I'd known Shaggy was going to be here I would never have invited Bree to join me. Normally, she was a mature, sophisticated woman, but Shaggy had a way of bringing out the child in her, and not in a good way.

"Oh good, you're here," Tony said as I entered the room.

"Did you find something?" I asked.

"I think I did." Tony typed a rapid string of commands. "I've been looking at all his files, and I think Pike's secret might date back to the establishment of White Eagle. Maybe even earlier."

"That fits the other clues I've come across, although you'd think a secret that old wouldn't still hold a lot of power. Most of the people who were around back then have passed on, although I suppose it might be something so shocking the descendants of whoever it was about might still have a stake in making sure it never got out." I leaned a hip against Tony's chair, placing a hand on his shoulder as I leaned in to get a closer look at the screen. "Any idea where we should look next?"

"If I had to guess it has to do with this."

An old map popped up on the screen. "What are we looking at?" I asked.

"It's a site map that provides claim lines and boundaries. If you look at this map," Tony pulled up another map just like the one we'd just been looking at, "and compare it to this," he went back to the original map, "you can see what I mean."

I shook my head. "No, I can't. They look the same to me."

"Hang on." Tony typed in additional commands, then got up from his chair. He took my hand and walked me across the room to where a screen twenty times the size of the one on the computer hung on the wall. "Take another look now that the maps are side by side."

It took me a minute, but eventually I saw what Tony meant. "The lines are different."

"Exactly."

"Okay, so what are you thinking that means?"

He walked closer to the screen and pointed to a claim, *Bloomfield*, next to one entitled *Weston*. Both maps were dated 1942, but there was no way to know without further research which had come first. "If you look here you'll see *Weston* now occupies at least half of *Bloomfield*."

"So maybe the claim with a larger portion associated with the Weston mine came later and Bloomfield sold part of his claim to Weston. Or maybe the other map, with a larger percentage belonging to Weston, came first and Weston sold part of his claim to Bloomfield."

"Yeah, maybe. I think it warrants further research, especially because this is the mine that made Hank Weston his millions."

"Are you suggesting Hank Weston poached part of the claim belonging to Bloomfield?"

"Maybe. We don't have all the facts yet, but it might behoove us to get them."

"Agreed. I brought the boxes with the maps and land deeds. Maybe you can find something there."

"I'll look at everything tomorrow. Maybe between what I've found on the computer and what Pike saved in the boxes something will emerge."

I was about to ask Tony about our plans to find him the perfect Christmas tree when I heard a loud crash from upstairs. I glanced at Tony and we both went running.

I could hear Tilly barking as additional crashes that scared the life out of me continued. I didn't know what had happened, but I was afraid it was really bad until Tony, who arrived in the kitchen ahead of me, started laughing. I skidded to a stop behind him and looked over his shoulder.

"What on earth happened?" I asked as I stood with my mouth open staring at Bree, who had an entire bowl of chow mein noodles dripping from her head, and Shaggy, who had what I imagined was the entire order of sweet and sour pork dripping from his face.

"Tony's degenerate friend tried to kiss me," Bree screeched.

"I didn't try to kiss you, Smurfette. You had a bit of sauce from the sweet and sour pork on your cheek and I reached over to wipe it off before you brushed it with your hair."

"Like hell. I know when someone is moving in for a kiss." Bree looked at me. "Can we go now?"

"Yeah." I suppressed a giggle. "I think we'd better."

Bree managed to wipe away most of the food that had been dumped over her head, but she was still wet and sticky from the sauce, so I offered her the parka I kept in my Jeep, which was a lot heavier and warmer than the dressy jacket she'd been wearing. Once we were headed back toward town I asked her exactly what had happened.

"I don't know," Bree groaned. "Shaggy has a way of pushing my buttons. He seriously has to be the most annoying person on the planet."

"Oh, I don't know," I countered. "I kind of like him."

"Yeah, well, you're not short, so he doesn't tease you," Bree snapped.

"Like I've told you a thousand times, he teases me, but I don't let it get to me, so he backs off."

"My sweater is probably ruined."

"I'm sure it is, but if I was reading the situation correctly it seems you were the one to start the food fight."

"I told you, he tried to kiss me."

"Even if that were true, you didn't have to throw our dinner at him."

Bree sighed. She leaned her head against the rest behind her and closed her eyes. "I guess you might have a point. He leaned in and I panicked. The bowl with the sweet and sour pork was sitting right there and I threw it at him before I could even consider the consequences."

"Are you sure he really wasn't just leaning in to wipe sauce off your face?" I asked.

"I'm sure. I know when someone is going to kiss me, and I can guarantee you, Shaggy had a lip-lock in mind."

Bree was probably right. I'd noticed in the past that Shaggy not only teased Bree but watched her like a hawk. Personally, I didn't understand the whole teasing-as-foreplay concept, but I suspected that was exactly what was going on with Shaggy, and possibly with Bree as well. She was the most pulled-together, sophisticated person I knew, but she tended to let

Shaggy—and, to some extent, Donny—pull her into ridiculous situations. Both of them were as immature as they came; apparently, Bree had a type.

"Did you know you had a letter in the pocket of your jacket?" Bree asked, as I turned onto the main highway.

"The letter I was trying to deliver to Pike on the night he died. I totally forgot about it."

Bree turned it over, then over again, studying the envelope. "There's no return address. Do you think we should open it?"

I hesitated. As a postal worker, I knew never to violate the privacy of those to whom I delivered mail, but Pike was dead, and I was curious what was inside. "I guess it would be okay if you opened it," I answered. "There's a penlight in the glove box."

Bree opened the glove box and found the small light. She opened the envelope and unfolded a single sheet of red paper.

"What does it say?" I asked.

"'Dear Pike:

'It is with deepest sympathy that I am writing to inform you that Patricia has passed away. I know the two of you have not kept in touch, but she made me promise to contact you upon her death to let you know she was releasing you from the promise you made to her all those years ago. The secret Patricia has kept close to her heart has weighed heavily on her mind. She knew her end was near and didn't want the secret to die with the two of you, so she shared it with me and asked me to inform you upon her death that the information contained within it was yours to do with as you choose.

Sincerely, Bethany'"

Bree looked at me. "Wow. I wonder what secret she's referring to."

Chapter 5

Friday, December 15

I contemplated the mystery of Pike's murder as Tilly, Tang, and I made our rounds the next morning. Someone had shot Pike. I suspected the motive was either the money it was rumored he had hidden in his cabin or the secret he'd kept for a whole lot of years but had recently become burdened by. There were several key items I considered to be clues, including the empty trunk, which I suspected may have contained Pike's cash, the letter from Bethany regarding a promise Patricia had asked of Pike many years ago, and the files and emails on Pike's computer combined with the maps and land titles I'd found in his home.

The envelope from the letter Pike had received hadn't had a return address, but the postmark told me it had been mailed in Billings. Tony might be able to track down a Bethany in Billings who was in some way related to a Patricia who knew Pike. He was really good at that kind of thing, although Bethany wasn't all that unusual a name, so there were probably dozens of people who'd come up in a search.

As for the secret Pike was keeping, Tony was already working on it, and knowing him, he'd most likely have news for me later today.

"Morning, Frank." I set my mailbag on the floor and released Tang from the pack so he could run around the police station for a few minutes before we continued on our route. "Looks like the White Eagle PD received some Christmas cards to brighten up this place." I tossed a pile of mail including several red and green envelopes on the top of his desk.

"This place could sure use some brightening up. I was just saying to Mike this morning, we should get a little tree for the counter. I think we may be the only building in town that didn't bother to put out any decorations."

"A tree would be nice, but you might want to take care of it yourself. Mike isn't the sort to want to decorate."

"I guess you're right. Mike is all business, all the time, lately."

That didn't surprise me in the least. Mike had left childhood behind when our dad had been killed and he'd had to take over as man of the house. He'd put aside his fun-loving ways and set his sights on taking care of whatever needed doing. It was kind of sad that he'd given up such a large part of his childhood to take care of Mom and me. "Is he around?"

"He's over at the courthouse."

"I thought Donny's arraignment wasn't until this afternoon."

"It wasn't, but Donny decided to take a plea deal. Mike's seeing to the details."

I frowned. "What kind of plea deal?"

Frank leaned forward slightly as Tang crawled up his leg. He picked up the kitten and set him on the desk before he answered. "It seems when faced with being charged with murder one, he came clean about the burglary."

I narrowed my gaze. "Burglary?"

"It turns out Donny did steal a whole lot of money from a chest in Pike's cellar. From what I understand, it amounted to more than a hundred grand."

I let out an involuntary gasp.

"As we suspected," Frank continued, "he used some of the money to pay off his debt to the moneylender."

"But he didn't kill Pike?"

Frank shook his head. "He swears Pike was already dead when he entered the cabin."

"Why didn't he report it?"

"He was there to steal money from him," Frank reminded me. "If he'd reported the murder it would have cast suspicion on him when it was discovered the money was missing."

"Oh. Yeah, I guess that makes sense." I bit my lip as I tried to wrap this whole thing around in my mind. "Are you sure he didn't kill Pike? I hate to think he did, but…"

"Mike spoke to Donny himself and feels certain he's telling the truth. The report from the medical examiner supports the fact that Pike had been dead for more than twenty-four hours when you found his body, and Donny was seen near Pike's Place earlier that same day."

"So, if Pike was already dead he couldn't have told Donny where the money was hidden. How did he find it?"

"Donny told Mike that Brick Brannigan let it slip that Pike kept a bunch of cash in his cellar. I'm not sure how *he* knew, but Brick and Pike were pretty close. I suppose it might have come up at some point."

"I can see how Pike might have shared the existence of the money with Brick, but why on earth would Brick share that with Donny?"

"According to what Donny said, Brick had been drinking and Donny asked just the right questions. Mike talked to Brick, who doesn't remember even having a conversation with Donny about the money, but he admitted to tying one on a few weeks back after receiving some bad news. Donny and a few others were at the bar after closing and he figures that must have been when Donny tricked him into saying what he did. Poor guy feels like hell for his part in the whole thing."

"Yeah, I guess so." I still wasn't totally convinced Donny's story was on the up-and-up, but Mike was a smart guy and if Donny had been lying he would have figured it out.

"I assume Donny will still be doing jail time."

"Oh, yeah. He's being transferred to Kalispell today, and he'll be doing some time in prison. Depending on the deal he works out, he could be looking at quite a few years behind bars."

I thought of Bree and cringed. "Does Bree know?"

Frank shrugged. "Not as far as I know, but someone might have called her."

"I should go to her." I turned to the door. "If Mike comes back have him call me."

On one hand, it was a good thing Donny wasn't going to face charges for Pike's death. On the other, he was going to do time in prison, and Bree wasn't going to be happy about that. I took a deep breath before entering the bookstore, preparing myself mentally for the explosion of anger I was sure to meet when I gave her the news that Donny wasn't coming home anytime soon.

"Oh good, you're here," Bree greeted me with a weak smile. "I hoped you'd be by before the arraignment."

"There isn't going to be an arraignment. Donny worked out a deal."

Bree sat down on one of the chairs she provided in the reading area. "A deal?"

I explained as succinctly as I could the details Frank had relayed to me. I braced myself for an explosion of anger or perhaps an onslaught of tears, but instead my news was met with sad resignation.

"Are you okay?" I asked.

Bree nodded. "I've been thinking about things and I realized somewhere along the way that Donny probably had stolen Pike's money to pay off his gambling debt. I guess I'm relieved to know he didn't kill an old man in the execution of the theft." Bree wiped a single tear from her cheek. "I'm sorry Donny's going to prison, but I realize Donny has been on a fast train to trouble for quite some time."

I took her hand in mine. "Yeah, I think he has. I'm sorry."

Bree looked at me with tears in her eyes. "I need to let him go," she whispered.

"Yeah, I think you do."

******

When I hadn't heard from Tony by the time I finished my route, I decided to call him to check in. Tony often lost track of time when he was working, and while he probably intended to call me, as he'd promised, he'd become distracted and forgotten. I was anxious to see what, if anything, he'd found in the file, and I also wanted to ask if he'd be willing to track down Bethany. Of course Tony didn't answer when I called the first time, which didn't surprise me in the least, so I left a message and set about feeding Tang and Tilly, then got ready for my dinner with Brady Baker.

I stood in front of my closet in indecision. This wasn't exactly a date, so I didn't want to go overboard and make things awkward, but he'd texted me the name of a nice restaurant, so I didn't want to show up underdressed either. After several minutes I chose a long wool skirt, knee-high dress boots with a low heel, and an angora sweater Aunt Ruthie had given me last Christmas. I rarely wore makeup but decided a light dusting of powder and a dash of mascara couldn't hurt. I was debating whether to add a touch of lip gloss when my phone rang. I looked at the caller ID: Tony.

"Sorry I missed your call. I was in the computer room."

"No problem," I said. "I was just checking in to see if you had any news."

Tony paused. "Actually, I had a few things to talk to you about. Can you come over?"

"I have a dinner date I should finish getting ready for. Is there something important you wanted to share?"

"I mainly wanted to talk to you about the maps you dropped off."

"Okay. What did you find?"

"I did some research and it seems the circumstances surrounding the discrepancy between the claim boundaries are suspicious at best."

I glanced at the clock. I needed to get going if I was to be at the restaurant on time, but I had to know the rest. "Suspicious how?"

"It appears that prior to taking over the portion of the Bloomfield mine, which was where Weston pulled out the gold that made him rich, he wasn't doing all that well. In fact, it looked like his mine was all but dried up. At first, I thought maybe Weston had inside information about the gold just on the other side of his own shaft and worked out a deal with Bloomfield, but it turned out that shortly before Weston took control of the rich vein, Bloomfield met with an accident and died."

"What kind of accident?"

"There was a partial cave-in while he was working one of the tunnels farthest away from Weston's claim. He was trapped and died. Shortly after, Weston began mining the tunnel closest to his own claim, where he eventually made a fortune."

"So you think Weston killed Bloomfield and stole his gold?" I realized.

"I would say there's a very good chance that was what occurred."

I paused to let that sink in. "Say that's true. Say Hank Weston somehow knew there was a rich vein of gold just on the other side of the dry tunnel he was working, so he arranged for Bloomfield to die in a mining accident, redrew the claim lines, then mined the area Bloomfield owned but hadn't yet worked. No one suspected anything, so he got away with it and made the seed money for his lumber operation, which made him a very rich man. Hank has been dead for a long time; how does that relate to Pike's death?"

"Pike told Barton he had a secret he'd been keeping for a very long time. We know Pike was a miner at the time Weston worked the mines; maybe he found out what happened, or at least suspected it. He seemed to have been compiling data that could serve as proof of the plot."

"That makes sense, but again, Weston is dead. He couldn't have killed Pike."

"Yes, but Hank Weston had three sons and eight grandsons, all of whom are very rich men."

"You think one or all of them knew their father's secret and when they heard Pike was going to expose his crime one of them killed him?"

"It fits."

I bit my lip. "Yeah, it does. I want to explore this idea with you further, but I need to go now."

"It can wait. Are we still going tree cutting this weekend?"

"We are. Will tomorrow afternoon, say around three, work? I promised to volunteer at the animal shelter until two."

"Three works fine. I'll make dinner if you can stay to help me decorate."

"It's a date. Oh, and before I forget, I found a letter someone named Bethany in Billings sent to Pike regarding the death of someone named Patricia. I don't have last names or addresses. I don't suppose there's any way you can track them down?"

"That's not a lot to go on, but I'll see what I can do."

"Thanks, Tony. You're the best."

******

Being twenty minutes late to your first unofficial date with the new hunk in town probably wasn't the best way to make a good impression. "I'm very sorry," I said as I slid into the booth.

"It isn't a problem. I went ahead and ordered a bottle of wine. I hope that was okay."

"That was fine. And again, I'm sorry to be late. It's just been one of those days."

"I ran into Bree today and she told me about your friend. Are you doing okay?"

It took me a minute to puzzle out the fact that by *my friend*, he was referring to Donny. Part of me wanted to assure him that Donny was far from being *my friend*, but I didn't want to seem petty, so I decided to comment briefly, then change the subject. "Donny and I weren't close, but he was dating Bree and she's my best friend, so I feel bad for her. We spoke briefly and I think she's going to be fine, but thank you for asking. On another note, I managed to distribute all the flyers for tomorrow, and I even rounded up three additional volunteers to help out in the morning."

Brady smiled. "That's great. You have a reputation for being a real go-getter and I can see that reputation is justified."

"Thank you. I try to do what I can. The clinic hasn't had a lot of publicity, but I think we'll do okay. I'd like to go over the specifics because you won't be around."

He took a piece of paper out of his shirt pocket. "I brought a list of all the animals currently being housed at the shelter. It's separated into columns. The first one is the animals currently available for adoption; the second is the ones who are in quarantine. I looked over the applications my uncle used and they seem fine to me, so I saw no reason to change them. If you've worked clinics in the past I assume you have a good handle on the types of adoptive homes I'm looking for."

"I do," I confirmed.

"I've arranged for coffee and pastries to be delivered for both the volunteers and the members of the community who come out for the clinic. Unfortunately, I won't be available until after two, so I'm hoping you won't have any problems or questions."

"We'll be fine. Everyone I asked to help has done clinics before, and it doesn't sound like you're changing anything. I'm sure we'll find some awesome homes for the dogs in your care."

The conversation paused when the waiter came to take our order. I chose a filet, Brady the salmon. The wine he'd ordered was delicious, and I found myself beginning to relax and enjoy the evening.

"So, tell me about yourself," I said as we began our salads. I figured I knew everything I needed to about the clinic but very little about the man.

"There's isn't a lot to tell. I grew up in Portland, the middle of five children. I attended college in Boston with the intention of applying to veterinary school on graduation. After four years of biology, anatomy, and a bunch of other ologies, I found I was less than certain about the direction my life was taking, so, on a whim, I joined the army. After my first tour I took a short break before reupping. It was at that point that my life's trajectory went slightly askew."

"What happened?" I asked.

"I met a woman named Sheila while I was vacationing in Germany. She was bright and funny, and I fell instantly in love with her. Sheila was living overseas on a student visa but was about to return to the States, so I changed my plan to do another tour, applied to veterinary school, and came back home. After graduating, I asked Sheila, who I was living with by that point, to marry me and she accepted. I knew my uncle wanted me to take over his practice in White Eagle, but Sheila made it clear there was no way she was living way out here in the wilderness. She had a friend in Chicago who knew someone who had an opening in an established practice. I wasn't sure I wanted to be one doctor among many in a large practice, but Sheila convinced me it was a great opportunity, so I told my uncle I was going to pass and took the job in Chicago."

"And then?" I asked, knowing at least part of the answer.

"And then I came home early one day to find Sheila in bed with the man she claimed was only a friend, and I realized she had moved to Chicago to be with him in the first place. He was married and not interested in a divorce, and Sheila seemed to think getting engaged to me would make him change his mind."

"She was using you the entire time?"

"It would seem. Anyway, I knew my life was a mess and, after looking at things objectively, I realized I'd made every decision since meeting Sheila to accommodate her. I broke off the engagement, quit my job, talked to my uncle, who thankfully still wanted me, and here I am."

"Well, I for one am very grateful you're here, but I'm sorry you had to go through all that to get here. It sounds awful."

"It wasn't fun, but I feel like I'm a better man for having taken the journey. So far, I love White Eagle, the people are awesome, and the practice is great. So, how about you?"

I took a sip of my water before I began. "My life has been boring compared to yours. I was born and raised right here in White Eagle. I have one brother, Mike, who's a member of the White Eagle Police. My father died in an accident when I was fourteen and my mom owns a restaurant with my Aunt Ruthie. I spend my weekdays delivering the mail and I have several hobbies I enjoy on the weekend."

"What sort of hobbies?" Brady asked.

"I like to hike in the summer and ski in the winter. I also volunteer at the animal shelter, as you know, and I usually attend book club at the Book Boutique on Wednesdays, although I've missed the last few meetings. You already know I'm in a pretty serious relationship with my dog, Tilly, and now with Tang."

"Any serious relationships of the human variety?"

"If you're referring to friendships I have a bunch, but if it's romantic attachments, not for quite some time now."

Brady seemed pleased with my response. I wasn't sure that meant much, but it was something. I was about to ask him about his hobbies when his phone buzzed. He looked at the screen and frowned.

"I'm sorry. I have to go. It seems a dog has been hit by a car. The driver of the vehicle is waiting for me at the clinic."

"Go. It's not a problem at all." I looked toward the kitchen. "I'll wait for our entrees, have them boxed up, and bring them to your place. We can eat when you're done."

"You wouldn't mind?"

"Not at all. Now go. There's a life depending on you."

I couldn't help but feel a bit of fear as Brady hurried across the restaurant and out the door. I supposed it was a good sign that the driver who'd hit the dog had brought him to the clinic, but being hit by a car was a serious matter that could very well lead to a lot of injuries.

By the time the food was ready and packaged up, I'd paid for it, and driven to Brady's place, he was just finishing up. The dog had been sedated and had a cast on her leg but didn't look too bad considering the ordeal she'd just gone through. "Is she going to be okay?" I asked.

He nodded. "The driver who hit her is from out of town and has no idea who the owner might be. You don't recognize her, do you?"

I took a closer look at the dog, who appeared to be a terrier mix. "No, she doesn't look familiar. I'm sure her owner will come looking for her. There's a local webpage where lost and found pets can be listed. I'll post to the page. If we don't find the owner that way, I'll put some flyers up around town."

"Thanks. I appreciate it. Our patient should sleep through the night. Are you still interested in dinner?"

"I am. I had everything packaged in microwavable containers. I'll heat them up if you want to grab some plates and utensils."

"It smells good and I'm starving."

"I guess one of the downsides to having a solo practice is that you're always on call," I said when our food had been heated and served.

"Being a one-man operation does have its challenges. One of the only things I liked about the clinic in Chicago was that I had regular hours and was only on call a few days a month. My uncle made it work as a single practitioner for a lot of years, but I'm talking to a friend about coming on as a partner. Running both the veterinary hospital and the animal shelter is a lot for one person, and having someone to share on-call hours will make it easier to have a personal life. Besides, if I'm going to commit to the search-and-rescue operation I'll need someone to cover when I'm not here."

"That's true. Having a partner would make things easier. It might be slow for two people over the winter, but in the summer I'm sure you'll be glad for the help. Has your friend been working as a veterinarian for long?"

"Lilly's been practicing for eight years. She's a fantastic doctor and a small-town girl at heart, so I think she'll fit right in."

"Housing in the area can be difficult. She should start looking right away."

"I have a guest room. I figured she can just stay with me until she finds a place."

I hated the part of me that didn't like that idea. Brady and I were just friends, and having his new partner stay with him in the short term made a lot of sense. So why, I asked myself, did I feel a tinge of old-fashioned jealousy?

Chapter 6

Saturday, December 16

"So, tell me all about Dr. Cutie," Amberley Wade whispered into my ear after I'd sent a prospective adoptive parent off on a walk around the indoor exercise track with the dog they seemed to have fallen in love with. Amberley was the daughter of Kurt Wade and the granddaughter of Austin Wade, one of Dillinger Wade's three children.

"I don't know him all that well. He only recently moved to White Eagle."

"I know that," Amberley huffed, "but I also know you had dinner with him last night, and it appears you've been put in charge of this little shindig in his absence. Which leads to my next question: Why isn't he here?"

"He had to attend orientation for the search-and-rescue team, so I offered to cover for him."

Amberley fanned herself with her hand in an overly dramatic fashion. "Woo-wee. A doctor and an S-and-R-team member. Talk about a catch. I'm assuming he's single? I hadn't heard anything about a Mrs. Dr. Cutie."

"He's single," I confirmed.

Amberley smiled. "Good." She looked around the room. "I'm not much of a dog person, but I may need to adopt one of these fleabags so I have a reason to come by on a regular basis."

I raised a brow. "Spending time with a man you're attracted to is a terrible reason to adopt a pet."

"I suppose it's a bit extreme, but with the scarce selection of datable men in this town, extreme measures might be warranted. Still, I suppose dealing with dog hair and slobber might not be worth it."

"Assuming you aren't here to adopt a dog, which I highly doubt, why are you here?"

Amberley pursed her bright red lips. "I told you, I thought Dr. Cutie would be here. I wanted to meet him. I figured I'd better jump right in before someone else got their claws into him. Do you know when he'll be back?"

"Later this afternoon."

"I don't suppose you could put in a good word for me with the doc? Talk me up a bit to spark an interest? Maybe introduce us to cut through any awkwardness that might arise from a first meeting?"

I shook my head. "Sorry. I gave up my matchmaking license just last week. Now, if you'll excuse me, I have applications to process."

"How about if I had some information you might be interested in? Would you be willing to trade a glowing introduction for a piece of juicy gossip?"

"I don't gossip."

"It's about that old man you've been running around asking about."

"Pike?"

Amberley nodded.

I hesitated. The last thing I wanted to do was introduce Brady to the biggest sex kitten in town, but Amberley was a Wade, so it was conceivable she could know something beneficial to my investigation.

"What do you know?" I asked.

"Will you help me get acquainted with the doctor?"

"I guess I can arrange an introduction." I sighed. The reality was, White Eagle was a small town and the two were bound to meet eventually anyway.

Amberley looked around. "Is there somewhere we can talk in private?"

I nodded. "Let me tell one of the other volunteers I'm taking a break."

I led Amberley to one of the offices in the back and motioned for her to have a seat. "Okay, what do you know?"

"It's not that I actually *know* anything."

I frowned.

"It's more that I noticed some unusual behavior I thought might be of interest."

"Go on."

"A couple of weeks ago I was at my grandfather's, visiting Fantasia. I was just leaving when a taxi pulled up with Pike Porter inside. I asked what he was doing so far out of town and he said he'd stopped by to speak to my grandfather. I asked Grandfather about it; he and people like Pike don't normally spend time together, and he said Pike just wanted to catch up on old times. That sounded like a flimsy explanation to me, so I spoke to Fantasia—she likes to snoop—and she said Pike and my grandfather had business to discuss, but she didn't have the details. The next thing I knew, Pike was dead. I find that curious. Don't you find that curious?"

"I do." I glanced at Amberley. "But why are you telling me this?"

"Because you promised to introduce me to the cute doctor."

"You do realize you may have just implicated your grandfather in Pike's death?"

"What?" Amberley looked at me with genuine surprise on her face. "My grandfather didn't kill him. I just said he'd had a conversation with him. So, will you introduce me to Dr. Cutie?"

After I once again promised Amberley I'd arrange for her to meet Brady, I sent her on her way. If Mike was correct that Donny had stolen Pike's money but hadn't killed him, the secret Pike was thinking about sharing with Andrew Barton was the only motive. Or at least the only one I was aware of. If anyone from the Wade or Weston family was involved in Pike's death it was going to be hard to prove. Between the two families, they owned most of the land in town and controlled most of the wealth. The Wades and Westons were about as close to royalty as you could get in this part of Montana.

"Please tell me Amberley wasn't here to adopt a dog," one of the other volunteers said after she left.

"No, she just wanted to meet the new bachelor in town. Did the woman who came to meet the collie mix make a decision?"

"She loves the dog and is filling out an application as we speak. Do you know if we're supposed to take drop-offs today?"

"Someone's here who wants to drop off a dog?"

"The man in the blue sweater standing next to the Ford truck."

"I'll talk to him. Why don't you check on the prospective adoptive parents who are walking on the exercise track?"

It always made me sad when people surrendered their pets to the shelter, but at times life situations demanded such a decision. Still, in my opinion there were those who took their relationship with their pets far too lightly. One man actually told me that when he'd brought home a puppy he had no idea dogs shed. Seriously? Had he grown up on another planet?

"I understand you have a dog you'd like to drop off?" I asked the man in the blue sweater.

"I do. I think he might be lost. I found him on the highway a good twenty miles out of town. I'm just passing through on my way to the East Coast, so I can't keep him. I figured he was better off with you than on the side of the highway."

"You were right, he is better off with us. Let me grab a leash and I'll take him off your hands."

The dog who had been brought in looked to be a shepherd mix. Not only was he a lot thinner than he should be, but he had open wounds on the bottom of his feet. He'd be better off in the animal hospital than the shelter, so I took him there while another of the volunteers held down the fort. I wasn't a veterinarian and didn't want to overstep, but I figured it wouldn't hurt to clean and wrap the wounds before housing him temporarily in one of the holding cages.

"Well, aren't you a sweet thing," I said as the dog sat and stared at me as I worked. I didn't know if he was always this mellow or if he was so exhausted from his travels that he didn't have an ounce of fight left in him. "I wish you could tell me whether you have people looking for you." The dog didn't have a collar, but he could have had one when he started out and lost it along the way.

I poured a dish of dog food and a fresh bowl of water, then set them in one of the large pens, along with a soft, heated dog bed. The look of gratitude on the dog's face when he sank into the soft folds of the warm bed made me want to cry.

"Now you have a good nap. Doc Baker will be back in a couple of hours and he can take a better look at those feet." The dog closed his eyes and drifted off to sleep.

As long as I was there, I decided to check in with the two other hospital residents, the dog who'd been brought in the previous evening looked to be doing much better, and a cat who'd been found with a broken leg. Both patients were resting comfortably, so I imagined Brady had given them light sedatives to help keep them quiet. The lights in the pen were dim and there was soft music playing in the background. I almost found myself wanting to curl up on one of the dog beds and take a nap myself.

By the time the clinic had wrapped up for the day we'd managed to find forever homes for half of the dogs in residence. I hoped the others would be placed once the prospective humans who'd shown interest in them had a chance to think things over a bit. The animals were all returned to their pens and the volunteers left, and I went back to the animal hospital to check on the patients. When I arrived there was a man waiting near the entrance. "Can I help you?" I asked.

"I understand a dog was brought in last night who'd been hit by a car."

"Yes. Is your dog missing?"

He nodded. "Chestnut. She somehow got out of the yard a week ago and I've been looking for her ever since."

"Can you describe your dog?"

"About forty pounds, long chestnut hair, soulful eyes."

I smiled. It sounded like he was describing a woman, not an animal, but his description fit the dog who'd been brought in exactly. "It does sound like your dog was brought in."

"Is she okay?"

"She's doing great. Doc Baker expects her to make a full recovery." I looked at my watch. "The thing is, he isn't here right now and I'm not authorized to bring anyone into the hospital. He should be back in an hour if you want to come back then."

The man shook his head. "I'll wait. I'm not leaving without my girl."

Unfortunately, he did have to leave without his girl. At least temporarily. When Brady arrived he happily reunited the man with his dog, but explained that due to the severity of her injuries, he wanted Chestnut to spend another day or two in the hospital. The man worked out a time to pick up his dog on Monday, then reluctantly left. I felt sorry for the guy, but I thought Brady's caution was warranted.

"Tell me about the shepherd," Brady said after the man left.

"A man found him on the side of the highway about twenty miles out of town. He's been resting comfortably since I brought him in. I wrapped his paws, but they're in pretty bad shape, so you'll want to look at them."

"I will." Brady turned on the faucet and began to wash his hands. "How did the clinic go?"

"Great. We found homes for about half the current shelter residents. How was the orientation?"

"Good. It appears White Eagle has a close-knit group I'm going to enjoy being a part of. I can't wait to get started. I explained that I needed to line up some help here at the clinic before I could commit to being on call, but until then, Tracker and I are considered part of the team and will be invited to train with them and attend team activities."

"That's awesome."

I watched as Brady unwound the bandages from the dog's paws and closely examined each one. The look of compassion on his face as he worked warmed my heart. After he methodically examined each paw, treated, and rewrapped it, he knelt down so he was on eye level with the animal and explained what the next few days were going to be like. I swear, it seemed as if he believed the dog understood.

"I should get going," I said after Brady settled the dog back on his bed. "I promised a friend to help him find a Christmas tree."

"Sounds like fun. Thank you again for all your help."

"No problem. I was happy to pitch in." I turned and started to leave. "I know this is kind of random, but my mom is making dinner for the family tomorrow afternoon. Would you like to come?"

Brady smiled. "I'd love to."

"Great. I'll text you the time and address."

******

By the time I picked Tang and Tilly up from my cabin and drove out to Tony's the sun had started to descend. I figured we had less than an hour of daylight left, but there were plenty of beautiful trees on his property, which meant we wouldn't need to drive anywhere to find the perfect fir. All we needed to do was choose one, cut it down, and haul it inside; then we'd have the whole night to decorate. I was anxious to find out if Tony had any news regarding Pike's murder and all the random pieces that seemed to be attached to it, but also excited to help Tony decorate his place. In all the years we'd been friends he'd done so much for me. Helping to brighten his living space would be my way of giving back to him a bit.

"What about this one?" Tony asked.

"Too tall," I answered. "It will be too hard to decorate. How about the one over near the road?"

"Too wide. I don't want to be running into the darn thing for the next two weeks." Tony walked up the hill we'd decided had the best selection through shin-deep snow. "How about this one?"

I considered the tree. It was a noble fir, about eight feet tall, which had grown full but cylindrical. "I think it's perfect. Let's get it inside and set up in the stand. We can eat first, then decorate."

"Stand?"

I narrowed my gaze. "You don't have a tree stand?"

Tony slowly shook his head.

I glanced at my watch. "The hardware store will be open for another hour. Let's head into town to pick up what we need. We'll just grab a pizza; it'll be faster than cooking. As long as we're at it, do you have lights?"

"I have lights," Tony confirmed.

"And ornaments?"

"Does it really need ornaments?"

I rolled my eyes. "Come on. We'd better hurry."

By the time we cut down the tree and dragged it onto the closed-in porch to dry out we had less than thirty minutes to get into town before the hardware store closed. I figured if we were in the door before six Hap wouldn't kick us out unless this was one of his date nights. Regardless, it was best to hurry, so I packed Tang and Tilly into the backseat of Tony's truck and we started into town.

"Talk to me about the case," I suggested as we sped down the mountain at a pace I wasn't entirely sure was safe on icy roads.

"Okay, let's talk about the case," Tony agreed as he hugged the side of the lane as he navigated a sharp curve. "I've looked at the maps, mine claims, and land documents extensively, and it seems certain to me that after the man's death, Weston mined Bloomfield's claim closest to his own and made a fortune. There's no way to know based on the information we have whether Weston caused the cave-in to gain access to the gold, or if he just took advantage of the accident. I suppose it's even possible

Bloomfield had worked out a deal with Weston before he died."

"So, despite the fact that we have a feasible theory as to Pike's secret, there's no way to figure out if this series of events is even related to Pike's death."

"Correct. Even if we could prove Hank Weston killed Bloomfield, then stole his gold, it won't help us in pinpointing Pike's killer. Hank Weston is dead, which would lead me to believe the killer could be a child or grandchild, but we'll need more to get anywhere with that line of thought."

"Maybe if we start by considering Hank Weston's descendants as suspects we can narrow things down."

"It might give us a starting point."

"I spoke to the new librarian, Wilma Cosgrove, the other day. She told me that Pike had been looking at old newspapers the week before his death. I have no way of knowing what he was looking for, though I found a newspaper in which Austin Wade's birth was announced. It was circled."

"You think Pike circled it?"

I shrugged. "I have no way of knowing who circled it, or even if it's relevant, but it seems interesting."

"I guess it's important to consider everything we find as a potential clue. We have no way of knowing what sort of secrets Pike might have been keeping. In fact, we don't even know if that's what got Pike killed. What we need is some sort of physical evidence to link the killer to the murder scene. Are you sure your brother didn't find anything?"

"As far as I know, nothing other than Donny's prints. He'll be at my mom's for dinner tomorrow. I'll see if I can soften him up to get him to tell me what he knows. It might help if I bring him the laptop."

"I'm done with it. I've copied what I needed into my own files." Tony slowed just a bit to navigate an icy patch and then continued. "As far as I can tell, other than a few emails, Pike only used the computer to play games and watch movies."

"I wondered why he even had a computer. He wasn't the sort to appreciate modern technology, but he was alone a lot, so having the computer to play games and watch movies makes sense. Did you find anything else at all?"

Tony sped up as we approached a flat, straight stretch of highway. "I wasn't able to track down the person who sent the letter to Pike, but he was married to a woman named Patricia back in the fifties. I didn't find anything suggesting they ever divorced, so I'm uncertain why she left him. I can keep looking for someone named Bethany in Billings. If Bethany and Patricia were just friends, the odds of my finding her are pretty remote, but if Bethany is a child or perhaps a grandchild, I may be able to find a link between them." Tony pulled into the lot behind the hardware store and we slipped out and headed inside. It was a quarter to six, so we'd need to hurry.

"What are you doing here so late?" Hap asked.

"Tony needs a tree stand and some ornaments."

"Have both, but you'll need to hurry. I'm closing in fifteen minutes and I can't be late; it's date night."

I looked at Tony. "You grab a stand and I'll grab some decorations."

"You've lived here a long time," I said to Hap as he led me to the aisle where the ornaments were kept.

"Most of my life."

"Do you remember someone named Patricia who was married to Pike?"

"Sure."

"Can you tell me anything about her?"

"She was a pretty little thing. She came here to help a friend who was pregnant, met Pike, and ended up staying."

"Do you know who the friend was?"

"A woman named Grace. Can't remember her last name. I think she left town shortly after she gave birth."

"So, Pike met Patricia when she came to White Eagle to help her pregnant friend, ended up staying, and eventually married Pike."

"That's what I just said."

"Yes, I guess it is." I began to stack ornaments into the basket I'd grabbed. "At some point she left White Eagle. Do you remember why?"

Hap shook his head. "Don't rightly know. It seemed she'd settled in just fine. She seemed to get along fine with Pike, and as the only midwife in town she'd made a lot of friends. She seemed happy enough, although it isn't like I knew her well. You might ask Bella Bradford about her, if you're really interested. Bella's a decade older than me and was closer to Patricia's age. Seems to me I remember them being friends."

"Okay, thanks. I'll try to track her down tomorrow."

Tony and I gathered together the things we needed for his tree, then went to the pizza parlor. It was crowded even for a Saturday night, but we managed to find a booth in the back. Tony went to the bar to get us beers while I looked over the menu.

"Was there a problem with the pizza?" Tony asked when he rejoined me at the table.

"No, I ordered a combo."

"Then what's with the frown?"

I offered Tony a weak smile. "Sorry. I guess I'm not much of a fun date. It's just that this thing with Pike is really frustrating me. I feel like I'm finding out a lot about him and his life, but so far nothing's pointing to a killer."

Tony placed his hand over mine. "Perhaps you should take a step back and let Mike and Frank figure out who killed Pike. It's their job, after all, and you only became involved in the investigation because Bree asked you to help clear Donny. Seems like that reason no longer exists."

"True," I admitted. "But my curiosity has been ignited, and it might be too late to walk away. Hap not only verified that Pike had been married to someone named Patricia, but that she was a popular midwife who seemed to have just up and left for no apparent reason. And then there's the letter from Bethany, letting Pike know Patricia had released him from some sort of a promise she'd asked of him. What was that all about? And if that isn't enough, there's the whole thing with the maps Pike had and the Bloomfield mine."

"It does seem like there was a lot going on."

"Right! Oh, and Amberley told me that Pike visited her grandfather shortly before his death. I don't know what's going on, but I feel like we're close to figuring everything out."

Tony shrugged. "Okay. We'll keep looking. Let's talk about a strategy to attack the problem while we decorate the tree. Maybe the answer is somewhere in the boxes you brought over from Pike's house."

"The letters," I blurted out.

"Letters?"

"When we were looking through Pike's things there was a stack of letters from Patricia. At the time I had no idea who Patricia was and they looked personal, so I set them aside. We need to go by Pike's place on the way out to yours. Hopefully, the letters are still there. If the secret Pike had been keeping had something to do with the woman who married and then left him, maybe we'll find something that will help pull everything together."

As it turned out, the letters were filled with chitchat about Patricia's life after she left White Eagle, with no mention of a secret or the reason she left town. Tony and I might have hit a dead end in terms of identifying Pike's killer, but we had an amazing time decorating his tree and sharing stories of Christmases past.

Chapter 7

Monday, December 18

Tilly and I trudged through the heavy snow as we made our rounds. I carried my mailbag and Tilly carried Tang in the backpack. Tang had grown quite a lot since he'd been having regular meals, and it wouldn't be long before Tilly and I would need to leave him at home. So far, Tang and Tilly seemed fine with the present setup, so I decided to allow Tang to come along with us until one or the other showed signs of discontent.

"Morning, Hap," I said as I tossed his mail on the counter.

"Best warm up by the fire. It looks like you have more snow on you than we have on the sidewalk out front."

"It's coming down pretty hard. Is it okay if I let Tang out of the backpack for a few minutes?"

"That'd be fine."

I lifted Tang from the carrier, then slipped the pack off Tilly's back. I figured all three members of White Eagle's mail-carrying team needed to dry out and warm up a bit.

"Did you get a chance to speak to Bella?" Hap asked.

"I called her, but she was busy yesterday. I'm going to stop by her place this afternoon. I'm hoping she'll have some insight as to why Patricia left and what promise she asked of Pike that was so huge she wanted to formally relieve him of his obligation on her deathbed."

"Coffee?" Hap held up an empty mug.

"Thanks."

He poured a cup and handed it to me. I took a sip and sighed as the hot liquid slowly worked its way through my body. I loved my job, but there were days, like today, when I found it a challenge as well.

"Hattie and I talked about your little investigation over Sunday dinner," Hap said. "She wondered if you knew about the Bloomfield mine."

"Sort of. I know the mine next to the one owned by Hank Weston belonged to someone named Bloomfield, who died in a cave-in. Somehow, Weston ended up with his claim, and the gold from the Bloomfield mine was what made his fortune."

"Sounds about right."

"Tony and I think one of Hank's descendants might be behind Pikes death."

"Kind of doubt anyone would care much about a claim jump that occurred so long ago."

"It's not just that. I think Pike threatened to tell the visiting historian that Hank Weston killed

Bloomfield to get his gold. Seems to me that even all this time later folks would care about that."

"Hank didn't kill Bloomfield."

"How do you know?"

"Pike told me as much. According to him, Hank Weston stole the gold from the mine after Bloomfield died, but the man who killed Bloomfield did it for love, not money."

"So, you're saying someone other than Hank Weston killed Bloomfield, which then opened the door for Weston to jump his claim and make a fortune?"

"That's exactly what I'm saying."

"It seems like this mystery keeps getting more and more convoluted."

"Seems that's the way with mysteries that stand the test of time. Those who know the facts die off, leaving only those who base their theories on tidbits of information that more often than not don't or can't form a clear picture."

"I guess you make a good point." I took the last sip of my coffee and set the mug on the counter. "In fact, the more we dig into this, the more certain I am that the secret Pike had been keeping close to his chest for so many years may have died with him." I picked up the backpack, which had dried out while we'd been talking. "If that's the case, the question I need to be asking is whether the secret had anything to do with Pike's death."

"I suppose there are a lot of reasons to kill a man. Some of them could have to do with what he knows, but it's just as likely someone killed him for another reason entirely."

I slipped the backpack onto Tilly's back. "I guess Tony was right; grasping for a motive will only get me so far. I need real evidence if I'm going to figure out why Pike died."

"Seems like you might want to talk to your brother about that," Hap suggested.

"I tried to talk to him yesterday, but he wasn't in a sharing frame of mind. I could tell he was concerned about something, however. The last time he had that look on his face was when he arrested Donny. I can't help but wonder who's next." I put Tang in the pack. "Okay, it looks like we're ready. The kids and I need to finish the route. I'll see you tomorrow."

"Try not to get too wet. There's a nasty flu going around."

As we continued the route, the snow definitely impeded our ability to get it done quickly, which meant we'd most likely still be walking the streets after dark if we didn't find a way to pick up the pace. I considered canceling my appointment with Bella so I could work through lunch, but I wanted to find out more about Patricia, so I firmed up my resolve and began to walk faster. After two hours of trying to make up time and getting nowhere I made two decisions: the first was to run Tang and Tilly home—they were both wet and looked miserable—and the second was to call Bella to see if I could move our appointment to the next day. She was fine with meeting on Tuesday, so I settled Tang and Tilly on the dog bed near the fire, then went back out into the storm, determined to complete my route before the shops began to close at the end of the day.

******

"You look like something the cat dragged in," Mom said later that afternoon as I entered the restaurant to make my final delivery.

"Long day, lots of snow, cold, and exhausted."

"Have a seat and I'll get you some hot coffee and a sandwich. Where are the kids?"

"I took Tang and Tilly home. It was too miserable a day for them." I took a sip of hot coffee that had never tasted better. "Your mail is in the bottom of my bag. I made you my last stop with the idea of doing just this, so everything in there should be yours."

"Oh good, more cards." Mom's face lit up. "Look at this, Ruthie, two from Ireland and one from Italy."

"The two from Ireland must be from the tour group that stopped in last fall," Ruthie replied.

"I think you may be right." Mom opened one of the cards. I couldn't help but notice the blush she quickly tried to hide.

"What is it?" I asked.

"Nothing, dear. It's just a nice card for our wall."

Ruthie grabbed the card out of her hand and looked at it. She glanced at my mom and grinned. "It looks like someone has an admirer."

"I don't have an admirer. Romero is barely an acquaintance. He's just a nice man with whom I happened to have a nice chat when he was passing through."

Ruthie chuckled. "If you say so." She passed the card to me. It was a beautiful card with a brief handwritten note.

"'Dearest Cara'?" I said aloud.

"Romero is Italian. The Italians are a passionate people. Can we please change the subject?"

I suppressed a smile as I handed the card back to my mother. I couldn't help but notice she slipped it into the pocket of her apron rather than hanging it on the wall with the other cards the café had received that day. My dad had been gone a long time and my mother was a beautiful woman, so I wasn't sure why I was so surprised she'd caught the eye of one of the many men who passed through each day.

"Looks like there's a letter for you mixed in with our mail," Mom said as she handed me a white envelope. It had my name and address on it, but no stamp or postmark.

Odd. Someone must have slipped it into my bag while I was making my rounds. I'd stopped several times to warm up, and each time I'd taken off my bag and set it on the floor, so there were any number of places the note could have been dropped inside without my noticing.

I opened the envelope and took out a single sheet of white paper. It was a typewritten note that said, *Secrets long buried are better off left buried.*

"What does it say, Tess?" Mom asked.

"It's just an invitation to a Christmas party," I said, not wanting to worry her.

"That's nice. It seems a lot of folks are having parties this year. I've been invited to four myself. Of course, I have my duties at the diner to consider, but I might try to fit one or two into my schedule. Would you like more coffee, dear?"

"No. I should get home. The kids will be waiting for their dinner."

As I made the short drive home, I tried to remember all the places I'd stopped that day. Someone must have been alone with my bag long enough to slip the note inside. The method of delivery seemed childish and inefficient. When I stopped to think about it, the note could have ended up mixed in with anyone's mail.

The envelope had been at the bottom of my bag. I supposed whoever put it there hoped I'd find it at the end of the day. Still, the whole thing reeked of high school.

I turned onto the highway, still wondering where the note could have been put in my bag. The most logical explanation was that someone had put it in before I loaded the day's mail and I just hadn't noticed it. There were only seven employees assigned to our branch of the post office. While it was possible any of the other six could have done it, the most likely were Jane Watson, a thirty-year veteran who worked the desk, or Luke Smith, a twenty-year veteran who worked the back room. I mentally considered each of my coworkers in relation to the motive they might have to send me the note. It seemed to me the secret referred to in the note was the same one Pike had been carrying around all these years.

I set the puzzle aside as I pulled into my drive. Tang and Tilly both acted like I'd abandoned them for weeks instead of hours. I put some soup on to heat because I was still hungry despite the sandwich Mom had made for me, then took Tilly out for a quick walk. When we returned I fed both animals, then settled onto the sofa in front of the fire to have my dinner.

God, I was tired.

I'd just finished my soup and was about to doze off when my phone rang.

"Hey, Bree; what's up?"

"I just wanted to touch base. You hurried in and dropped off today's mail before I was even able to say hi."

"I wanted to get my route done before dark and with the storm it was looking unlikely, so I didn't stop to chat. I have time now, however." I got up, picked up my bowl, and started toward the kitchen. "I didn't see you all weekend. How are you doing?"

"If you mean how am I doing with the fact that the man I thought was the love of my life stole an old man's life's savings to pay off a gambling debt and will most likely spend a whole lot of years in prison, fine. Don't get me wrong; there are moments when total disbelief sets in and I'm numbed by the absurdity of it all, but looking back, I can see Donny was never really the man I thought he was. Before this happened, I would have sworn I wasn't the sort of woman to be so taken with a man that she couldn't see his shortcomings, but as it turns out, I was wrong. That's exactly the sort of woman I am."

"Don't beat yourself up. Donny had a charm he used to cover up his true personality. I was fooled too for a while. I think the best thing you can do is to put this behind you and move on with your life."

"You're right and I will. As soon as I'm done wallowing in self-pity."

I laughed. "Wallow all you want. I believe ice cream is the regularly prescribed remedy for a broken heart. I'd invite you over to have some, but I'm all out."

"Ice cream is the last thing I need. Now that I'm back on the market I need to watch my calories. By the way, how did dinner go last night?"

"It was nice. My mom loved Brady, as did Mike. We had a lovely meal and everyone got to know each other a little better. Mike was impressed that Brady signed up for the search-and-rescue team and the two of them spent most of the afternoon discussing past rescues and new equipment. It was a very relaxing and pleasant day."

"So, are you going after him?"

"Going after him? What am I, twelve?"

"You know what I mean. Do you plan to pursue him as a sexual partner?"

"Geez, Bree, that's a little personal even from a best friend."

"So, you *are* going to pursue him?"

I paused before answering. "I'm not pursuing anything. Brady and I are friends. He happens to get along well with my family, so I'm sure I'll invite him to Sunday dinner again, and I plan to volunteer at the shelter on Saturdays, so we'll be spending some time together there, but at this point there'll be no pursuing, sexually or otherwise."

"But you like him?" Bree prodded.

"Yes, I like him. I like a lot of people. Now can we change the subject?"

"'Tess and Brady sitting in a tree…'"

"Geez, Bree, have you been drinking?"

"A little bit," she admitted. "Don't worry; I'm not going out and I've only had enough to take the edge off my misery, which I assume is the exact amount it takes to bring out my silly side. I'm sorry. Let's talk about something else, as you suggested. Are you still looking in to Pike's death now that saving Donny is off the table?"

"I am, but I'm not having a lot of luck."

"Well, I may know something that will help. It's actually the reason I called you in the first place, but then the whiskey took over and I got sidetracked."

"Okay; what do you know?"

"Rita Carson came into the bookstore today and we got to talking about Pike's death. She said she'd seen Austin Wade's car in the parking lot in front of Pike's cabin the day before you found his body."

"Did she know why he was there?"

"She said she didn't. She just remembered seeing the car."

Tang jumped into my lap as soon as I settled onto the sofa. I scratched his neck and he began to purr. "It sounds like Austin being at Pike's on the day he died could be a real clue. The first real clue we've had, in fact. Did Rita say anything else?"

"Nothing that seemed important or relevant. She talked a bit about the mayor's gala, but that was about it. You can stop by to talk to her tomorrow to see if she has anything more to say."

"I think I'll do that."

We spoke for a few more minutes and then I called Tony. He didn't answer, so I left a message, then went into the bathroom to take a hot shower and get ready for bed. When I came out dressed in my footie pajamas, Tony was sitting on my sofa talking to Tilly.

"What are you doing here?" I asked, crossing my arms over my well-covered breasts.

"I saw I'd missed your call. I was in town, so I stopped by. The door was open."

I looked down at the one-piece outfit that was superwarm on a cold, blustery night but looked like something a toddler would wear. It momentarily crossed my mind to be embarrassed, but then I decided the heavy garment wasn't at all revealing, and I'd certainly seen Tony wear odder things.

"Why were you in town?" I asked as I sat down on the sofa next to him, curling my legs under my body.

"I was hanging with Shaggy. He was asked to test a new video game that will be coming out next year and he invited me to join him."

My face fell. "You didn't call me?"

"We did call you. Check your messages."

Sure enough, there were missed calls from both Tony and Shaggy. "It's been a long day. I'm sorry I missed it. It's been a while since we all got together to play."

"You didn't miss anything. The game is a dud. I hope the company takes our suggestions. If they don't I think they're going to end up losing a lot of money. So, why did you call me?"

I pulled a blanket over my lap because I was still cold despite the fire that burned brightly in the fireplace, the hot shower I'd taken, and my footie pajamas. "I hadn't talked to you since Saturday, so I wanted to see if you had any news."

"Not really. I may have narrowed in on the woman who sent the letter about Patricia. I need another day or so to know for certain. It seems we have a lot of information but nothing even resembling a smoking gun. Did you ever sit down with Mike to compare notes?"

"No. I was going to on Sunday, but he wasn't in a sharing mood, and Brady Baker was there, so I never had the chance to grill him. I'll talk to him tomorrow. If he seems open to a discussion I may even invite him to dinner this week. Are you free to join us if I can arrange it?"

"I'm always free for you, love."

I smiled. Tony really was the sweetest person. "I know you just finished playing a video game with Shaggy, but it's been a long day and I need to unwind a bit. Are you up for a quick game of World Domination?"

"I'm up for it if you don't mind losing."

Chapter 8

Tuesday, December 19

The snow had stopped by the following day, leaving a blanket of white covering the landscape. I glanced toward the ski area on the nearby mountain, wishing I had the day off so I could get in a few powder runs while the snow was fresh. Another storm was predicted for later in the week, so maybe there'd be powder conditions again by the time the weekend rolled around.

"Morning Tess, Tilly," Hattie greeted as we entered the bakeshop with the mail. "I see you're still carrying the kitten around."

I tossed a pile of mail on Hattie's counter. "Yeah. He's old enough to stay home now, but I haven't quite figured out how to make the transition. I don't think he's going to be happy staying home alone if Tilly and I both leave."

"Seems to me," Hattie said as she pushed a blueberry muffin still hot from the oven in front of me, "you're either going to have to leave Tilly home as well or you'll need to get a second kitten to keep Tang company."

I broke off a corner of the muffin and put it in my mouth. "I'd hate doing my route without Tilly, but I suppose a second kitten might be doable. Taking Tilly along with me wherever I go is pretty easy, but as Tang gets older it will be harder to bring him along as well. Brady mentioned he was expecting the arrival of a litter of kittens at the shelter when I spoke to him on Sunday, so maybe I'll stop by there after work."

"Seems like it might be a good idea. The new vet seems to be settling in right nicely. Everything I've heard from those I've spoken to has been positive."

"Brady's a great guy. It seems obvious to me that he really cares about animals, and he and his dog Tracker are going to join the search-and-rescue team. White Eagle is lucky to have him."

"I spoke to Bree, who seems to think the two of you might be an item."

"Bree doesn't know what she's talking about. Brady and I are just friends."

"Figured. I always thought you and Tony might make a go of it."

"Tony? Why would you say that? Tony and I are just friends. Have been for years."

"Maybe that's true, but the nerdy little kid who moved to White Eagle has grown into quite a good-looking man with a brilliant mind and a wad of money to boot. If I were you and I was interested in a relationship with him that amounted to something more than friendship, I wouldn't want to wait too long."

I picked up my pack and slipped it onto my shoulder. "I promise you, Tony and I are just friends. It's all we ever have been and all we ever will be. Thank you for the muffin, but I have a route to do. I'll see you tomorrow."

Tang, Tilly, and I continued down the street. The walkway had been shoveled, but it was still slippery, so we took it slow. "Why on earth would Hattie think Tony and I were anything other than friends?" I asked Tilly.

She barked, either in response to the question or to hearing Tony's name.

"Sure, he's a really good guy who always has my back, and, given all the hiking, skiing, and wood splitting, he's filled out quite nicely from the tall but stick-thin seventh grader I first met, but the idea of us as a couple is absurd."

I glanced at Tilly, who was trotting along beside me. "Am I right? The idea is nuts."

Tilly didn't say anything, but I had the oddest feeling she agreed with Hattie. I decided on the spur of the moment to stop in to talk with Brick. Rita had told Bree that she'd seen Austin's car in the parking lot near Pike's Place on the day he died, although it was just as likely Austin had been at the bar as it was he'd been visiting Pike.

"I guess I must have mail today," Brick greeted me. "Been awhile since anyone sent mail to the bar."

"Actually, I don't have mail for you, but I do have a question. I've been told Austin Wade's car was parked in front of Pike's Place on the day he died. Do you remember if he came in here?"

"He never comes in here. I guess we aren't upscale enough for his fancy tastes. And I don't remember seeing his car. Guess you could ask some of the other merchants. Once I come inside I rarely go into the lot unless I have trash to dispose of. Even if his car was in the lot I most likely wouldn't have seen it."

"Okay, thanks. I was just curious because you remembered seeing Donny's car."

"That was a fluke. Donny just happened to be parked in the lot when I went outside to meet one of the dealers dropping off beer kegs. I most likely wouldn't have noticed at all except that it was a slow day and the lot was mostly empty."

I thanked Brick again and went on my way. I'd need to pick up the pace if I was going to make my meeting with Bella Bradford.

******

Bella lived in a cheery home not far from Bree's. I didn't want to leave Tang and Tilly in the Jeep too long even though they were both tired out and sleeping peacefully in the cargo area, so I rang the bell intent on a quick but hopefully fruitful interview. Bella invited me in and we got settled and I dove right in with my first question.

"Did you know Patricia well when she lived here?" I asked as soon as we'd established the fact that they'd been acquainted.

"As well as anyone. During her time helping her friend she got to know many of the women in White Eagle and decided to stay. We didn't have a hospital back then, so many of the women elected to have home births. Patricia's services were very much needed and appreciated."

"I understand she and Pike married at some point."

Bella nodded. "They did. They seemed happy enough, but it didn't seem to me they shared a great passion as much as a deep and abiding friendship. Still, it appeared it worked for both of them and they seemed to settle in as a married couple just fine."

"Do you know why she left?" I asked.

Bella hesitated. She furrowed her brow as she seemed to consider the question. I waited patiently until she was ready to speak, and when she did, she spoke slowly and carefully. "I can't say as I know for certain what caused her to leave, but I do remember when it occurred. Patricia was a very good midwife who seemed to have an excellent record for healthy deliveries. I'm sure she must have lost a baby or two along the way—it wasn't uncommon for women to suffer complications that led to disastrous results in those days—but while she'd been in White Eagle she hadn't lost a one. At least until Emily."

"Emily?"

"Emily Brown was no more than eighteen. She was pregnant with her first child and was happier about her impending motherhood than anyone I'd ever seen. She was the sort of girl who drew you in with her smile. Everyone in town loved her. Anyway, Emily went into labor a couple of weeks early, which wouldn't have been a problem except that Bella was up at the Wade home, delivering Alberta Wade's oldest son. Alberta had been having problems since the beginning of her pregnancy and Bella didn't want to leave her alone, so when Emily's husband, Tom, came to tell her that Emily had gone into labor early, she assured him first pregnancies had long labors and she'd be by as soon as Alberta's baby was delivered. The problem was that Alberta's delivery took longer than she'd predicted, and by the time she made it to the home Emily shared with her young husband both Emily and her baby were in distress. In the end, both Emily and her baby died."

I put my hand to my mouth. "Oh God. The poor woman. Her poor husband." I took a breath and let it really sink in. "Poor Patricia."

"It was a dark time for the town. Emily had been so full of life and was such a popular figure. Everyone in White Eagle mourned for her. Not long after the funeral Tom left the area and life went on. I'm not sure why Patricia took Emily's death as hard as she did, but it seemed to haunt her. She slipped further and further into a dark depression and eventually, she returned to the home she'd left when she came to White Eagle in the first place. I never saw her again."

"Wow," I said as I fought my own tears. "That was quite a story. I guess I can understand why she might feel the need to get away. Thank you for sharing the story with me."

Bella put her hand over mine. "I was happy to help. Pike was a good man who lived a lonely life after Patricia left. I hope you find out who killed him."

Tilly, Tang, and I went on my route. We were making good time this afternoon and I hoped we'd be done early. The idea of getting a second kitten so Tang would have a companion was growing on me.

I'd called and talked to Brady, who said he had four kittens looking for homes.

I'd just finished my delivery to Sisters' Diner when my phone rang. It was Tony. "Hey, what's up? Are you still licking your wounds from the lashing I gave you last night?"

He laughed. "We both know I let you win so you wouldn't be aggravated after the long day you'd had."

"There's no way you let me win," I said, even though I knew it was true. "I not only beat you, I slaughtered you."

I could imagine the twinkle in Tony's eye as he responded. "I don't suppose we can keep that to ourselves? I do have a reputation to uphold."

"Yeah right. I doubt you called me to beg for my mercy."

"I found Bethany in Billings."

I stopped walking. "You did? Did she know Patricia's secret?"

"She said she did, but she wasn't comfortable sharing it over the phone. She wants to meet us before she decides whether to tell us what she knows."

"Billings is over four hundred miles away. It's not like we can just pop down there after work," I pointed out.

"Actually, we can if you aren't busy. I called my pilot and he's free to take us there and bring us back this afternoon. What time do you get off?"

"Pilot? You have a pilot?"

"There's a private air service I use when I need to meet with my clients. I know you think I sit around all day playing video games, but the truth of the matter is I travel frequently. How about it? Are you free?"

"I should be finished with my route between three-thirty and four. I'll need to run the kids home first. Do you want me to meet you at the airport?"

"I'll arrange for the jet to pick us up at four-thirty and pick you up at your house. I'll call Bethany and arrange to meet with her at six-thirty. We can have a late dinner after we get back."

"Okay. I'll see you then. And thanks, Tony. For everything."

"No problem. Your mystery is my mystery."

******

The flight to Billings was fabulous. I'd never traveled by private jet before and had been expecting something small, with room for only a couple of passengers, but the jet Tony had hired was not only big, it was luxurious. There was room for at least ten passengers if all the plush chairs and sofas were occupied, and a fully stocked minifridge as well.

"I guess I knew you must have to travel for work, but I never imagined you traveled like this," I gasped as we settled in for takeoff. "This sofa is more comfortable than the one in my living room."

"I don't like to be away from home for longer than necessary, so I've found a private service is the way to go. Would you like a drink?"

"Do you have a cola?"

Tony opened the minifridge. "Glass with ice or can?"

"Can is fine." I took it from Tony. "Did you ever get around to finishing your tree?"

"I did, and it looks fantastic. Shaggy came by with some *Star Wars* figures we added to it. By the way, I had a chat with Shaggy about teasing Bree. I felt bad about the way things went the other night. Shaggy now understands that harassing my guests isn't going to be tolerated, so I'm hoping we won't have a repetition of the great Chinese food fight."

"Thanks for talking to him, but I should have called before I popped over with Bree. I wouldn't have invited her along if I knew he was going to be there. I've never seen anyone get under Bree's skin the way Shaggy does."

"They do seem to bring out the worst in each other. Did you meet with Bella Bradford today as planned?"

"Yes. She told me a very sad story, but I'm not sure how it could possibly pertain to Pike's death. At first, I thought the motive for his murder might have been monetary, but Donny confessed to stealing the money but not to the murder. Then I thought the motive might have had to do with the fact that Hank Weston jumped the claim of a dead man and made a fortune, but he's dead, and from what Hap told me, it didn't seem there were any hard feelings anyway. And Hap said Pike told him that Bloomfield was killed over love, not money. I don't know what that means, but I suppose the secret Pike hinted at to Andrew Barton could have to do with Bloomfield's death. It sounds like Bethany knows the secret, or at least one of the secrets, Pike had been hanging on to. Maybe we'll have a clearer picture after we speak to her."

"Have you considered that whoever killed Pike did so for a reason completely removed from the claim jump, Bloomfield, or the secret Pike had been hanging on to?" Tony asked.

"Yes, it has. If that's true, however, I have no idea where to start. I'd hoped to talk to Mike about it on Sunday, but that didn't work out. I guess I can try again tomorrow if whatever Bethany has to say doesn't pan out."

"Don't worry, we'll figure this out," Tony assured me. "Better buckle up for landing."

"Already? It seems like we just took off."

"This jet is one of the fastest on the market. I have a car waiting for us when we land. We should have our answers within the hour."

The next hour flew by as we landed, were escorted to the car Tony had hired, and traveled to Bethany's home. Bethany Latham was Patricia's granddaughter. The first thing we discovered was that Patricia was pregnant with Pike's daughter when she left White Eagle. She'd informed Pike of his impending fatherhood, but he was unwilling to leave White Eagle and Patricia was unwilling to return, so they'd lived their lives separated by no more than a day's drive.

"Thank you for agreeing to meet with us," I said after Bethany showed us to a small seating area that at one time would have been referred to as a parlor.

"When my grandmother told me her secret, she assured me the information was mine to do with as I saw fit. She didn't ask me to keep her secret only to hold it as she passed into the next life. I knew Pike knew it too, so I figured I'd leave the burden of telling or not up to him, but then, when Tony told me that he'd been murdered, I realized it might very well be time for this secret to be brought into the light. The thing is, the secret, in my opinion, has the potential to hurt people currently living in White Eagle. If I'm going to pass it on I want to be sure it's to someone who'll handle the information with delicacy and respect."

"I understand," I said. "I'm not sure the secret Pike was keeping is even behind his murder, but the timing of his speaking to the historian and his death seems to be more than just coincidence."

"I agree, which is why I said I'd meet with you. Can I ask how it is you knew Pike?" Bethany asked.

"He's been living in White Eagle since long before I was born. I knew who he was—everyone does—but I didn't know him well until I began delivering his mail. My dog Tilly, who comes on the route with me, absolutely loved Pike, so we'd stop to chat whenever he had mail. Over time we began spending more time together. He liked to talk about the past and Tilly and I enjoyed listening to his stories. The last time I brought mail to him it was the letter you sent, informing him of Patricia's death. That was the day I found him dead."

"I'm sorry. That must have been horrible."

I nodded.

Bethany took a moment before speaking. "If I tell you what I know, do you promise to give thought to what you'll do with it?"

"I will. I want to find out who killed Pike, but I'm not interested in stirring up controversy if I don't have to. Based on what I know, it seems this secret has been buried for a long time, and long-buried secrets sometimes are best left that way." I frowned as I remembered the note I'd found in my mailbag. I still didn't know who'd sent it.

Bethany looked at Tony. "And do you promise to handle the secret with the care it deserves as well?"

"I do."

Bethany took a deep breath and let it out slowly. "Okay. I have a good feeling about the two of you, and to be honest, Patricia's secret is one I'd just as soon pass on responsibility for."

Tony and I sat quietly. I could see it was important to let Bethany set the pace, and I imagined Tony realized that as well.

"My grandmother first went to White Eagle to assist a friend who was pregnant. Grandma was a midwife and the friend had already suffered two miscarriages, so she wanted to improve the odds of her having a successful delivery. After the baby was born the friend moved away, but Grandma decided to stay. She met Pike and they were married and, based on what she shared with me, she was content with her life as both a midwife and a wife."

Bethany paused before continuing. "The problem occurred when two of her clients went into labor at the same time."

"Alberta Wade and someone named Emily Brown," I supplied.

"You know that part?" Bethany asked.

"A friend of Patricia's told me part of the story, but please continue."

"As I said, two of my grandmother's patients went into labor at the same time and, unfortunately, both had complications. There wasn't a hospital in White Eagle back then, or even a full-time doctor. When Emily's husband came to tell Grandma she had gone into labor, she already had her hands full with Mrs. Wade, so she told him she'd come as soon as Mrs. Wade delivered. As it turned out, Grandma was tied up a lot longer than she'd thought she'd be, and by the time she arrived to help Emily she was in a great degree of distress."

"Bella told me both the mother and child died," I supplied.

"Yes, that was the story, and the root of the secret. You see, both Mrs. Wade and Emily had sons. Mrs. Wade survived, but her baby died. Emily died while delivering her son, and Mr. Wade convinced my grandmother to give him Emily's child, which he presented to his wife as her own child."

"Wait. What?"

"Mrs. Wade had been given a sedative after her baby was born. She never knew he'd died as a result of the difficult labor. When she awoke her husband greeted her with a baby boy and she never knew the difference."

"What about Emily's husband?" Tony asked.

"He knew his wife had died during the delivery and was grief-stricken. When he was later told his son hadn't made it, he didn't question it. He buried his wife and the body of the baby he was given and left the area."

"Oh my God," I gasped. "How could she do that? What could Dillinger Wade possibly have said to convince Patricia to go along with the lie?"

"Emily's husband was a poor man who drank too much. Mr. Wade convinced my grandmother that the baby would have a better life with him and his wife. Grandma worried that Emily's husband wouldn't be able to provide a stable home life now that his wife was dead, so she let Mr. Wade talk her into agreeing to the switch."

"And the baby's father…did he ever find out the truth?"

"My grandmother never heard from him after he left White Eagle and had no idea what had become of him."

I glanced at Tony, who looked as shocked as I felt. "The baby who was switched at birth must be Austin Wade."

Bethany nodded.

"Do you know if Alberta Wade ever found out that the baby she raised wasn't her own?" I asked.

"Grandma didn't know."

Wow.

Both Dillinger and Alberta Wade were dead, as were Pike and Patricia Porter. Emily's husband had been out of the picture for a long time and could be dead by this time as well. In my mind, the only one alive who could still be hurt if the truth came out was Austin Wade. I remembered seeing his birth announcement circled in the newspaper. It seemed as though Patricia had told Pike the truth at some point, so it didn't make sense that he'd been the one who'd looked it up and circled it. I hadn't been looking for a death announcement for Emily or her baby when I'd leafed through the newspapers, but now I wondered if it might have been recorded in the same weekly edition.

Tony and I thanked Bethany and went back to the airport for our return flight.

"What on earth are we supposed to do with this information?" I asked when we were in the air.

"I'm not sure. Do you think Austin Wade knows the truth?"

"Short of asking him, I don't see how we can find out."

"So, the question is, do we ask him?"

"If Austin knows the truth and killed Pike to keep the secret, we need to tell someone what we know. But if Austin never found out and wasn't responsible for revealing long-buried secrets we'd just be hurting an innocent man." I looked directly at Tony. "While I can't claim to know whether Austin knows he isn't a Wade biologically, I think someone does. Austin's car was seen in front of Pike's cabin on the day he was murdered and the note I found in my bag warned me that secrets long buried were best left buried. Unless there's another life-changing secret floating around, I have to assume someone knows the secret behind Austin's birth."

"Note in your bag?" Tony asked.

"I guess I forgot to tell you about that; someone left a note addressed to me in the bottom of my mailbag with that warning."

Tony frowned. "A threatening note seems like a pretty serious thing to forget to tell me about."

"The note wasn't threatening exactly, and I'd had a long day. By the time you showed up I was ready to forget about everything and just relax. I think the important thing to remember is that Rita Carson told Bree she'd seen Austin's car in front of his house the day he died."

"Sounds incriminating."

"So, what now?" I asked.

"The first thing we're going to do is find out who put the note in your bag. Chances are if we find that person we'll find the killer."

Chapter 9

Wednesday, December 20

As it turned out, Tony was wrong. I had Mike pull the prints off the paper the note was written on, and it turned out the person who'd slipped the note into my bag was none other than my co-worker, Jane Watson. When I asked her why she'd done it, she explained she knew I'd been running around town talking to people to uncover some deep, dark secret and was afraid I was going to uncover *her* deep, dark secret in the process. When I asked her what it was, she'd blushed and declined to say. I suspected Jane had been stepping out on her husband of more than thirty years, and I asked her point-blank if that was the secret she'd been trying to hide. She admitted it was. I had no reason to think she was Pike's murderer, so I let it go.

Tony and I decided our next move would be to talk to Austin Wade. We weren't sure what, if anything, he knew, but it seemed all threads in our investigation led to the man who wasn't a Wade at all. Tony called him to make an appointment for us to see him as soon as I finished my route on Wednesday. To speed things up a bit, Tony met me in midroute to take Tang and Tilly home.

The Wade home was more like a mansion. Austin was the oldest of the three Wade offspring so, while all of Dillinger Wade's sons were rich, Austin controlled the bulk of the fortune.

"How can I help you?" Austin asked after showing us to his office and offering us a seat.

I wished I'd rehearsed what I was going to say because I was suddenly tongue-tied.

Fortunately, Tony jumped in. "We're here to speak to you regarding a matter we believe might be related to Pike Porter's death."

"I see. And what matter might that be?" Austin, who owned his power and presented a strong, assertive posture, asked.

"We understand Pike came to see you several days before his death," Tony continued.

"That's correct."

"Do you mind if we ask what it was he wanted to discuss with you?" I asked.

"Given the fact that you aren't a cop or a representative of the Porter estate, I'm not sure what business it is of yours."

"We spoke to Patricia Porter's granddaughter," I said. "She explained the specifics of your birth."

Austin's lips pursed and his eyes narrowed. "In that case, I guess you're aware Mr. Porter knew something about me that I'd prefer didn't become public knowledge. I imagine you also suspect I killed him to keep him quiet."

"Did you?" I asked.

"No, I didn't. When Pike called to speak to me I suspected he wanted to talk about the secret that has overshadowed me for much of my life, so I agreed to meet with him. He said he was an old man and had carried the secret as long as he could and needed to unburden himself before he died. I assured him that I knew my father had convinced his wife to falsify the birth record so it would appear I was born to Dillinger and Alberta Wade, not to the young couple who were my real parents. My father had confessed the circumstances surrounding my birth to me years earlier, when we spoke hours before his death. Pike and I discussed the matter in depth and agreed a secret such as the one he and I had been asked to keep was too big to bear comfortably. Since my conversation with Pike I've shared that secret with both my brothers."

"How did they take it?" I asked.

"Better than I expected. As the eldest Wade son, I was given control of most of the Wade fortune. I suppose my brothers could make a case that because I'm not a Wade by blood, that control should go to the second son, my brother Jonathan, but my brothers agreed that while I may not have been a Wade by birth I became one by circumstance and should continue in my role as trust administrator."

"Thank you for your honesty. I'm sure the secret has been a great burden to you. I have one final question. If Pike and you spoke the week before, why did you visit him on the day of his death?"

"I didn't visit him. In fact, I was out of town at a conference that whole week."

I didn't argue. Brick had said he'd seen Austin's car outside Pike's on the day he died, but it seemed ridiculous for Austin to lie because his alibi was easily verifiable.

"I'm not sure whether the ramifications of the actions taken by my father and Pike's wife would be as great today as they were at the time of my birth, but I'd like to keep my dirty laundry within the family," Austin added as Tony and I stood up to leave.

"That's understandable. Tony and I won't say a word. Thank you again."

Back in Tony's car, I took a minute to process everything. In the past couple of weeks, I'd learned that Hank Weston had stolen a dead man's gold, though no one presently living seemed to care about it. I'd also learned that Dillinger Wade had made a deal with Pike's wife that at the time could have had huge ramifications, but now that everyone involved was dead, it had been reduced to no more than a mild embarrassment. The note that had been slipped into my mailbag, which had seemed like a huge clue had ended up being nothing more than a middle-aged woman trying to hide her affair from her husband.

Tony and I had uncovered a lot of dirty linen, but we still didn't know who killed Pike.

"Where does this leave us?" I asked as Tony started the car.

"I was about to ask you the same question."

"I wonder why Rita would lie about seeing Austin's car at Pike's on the day he died."

"Maybe she didn't lie. Maybe she was just confused." Tony turned onto Main Street so I could retrieve my Jeep. "I need to be home for a conference call in a little over an hour. Do you want to come over? I have a new video game."

******

I fed the animals, then changed into jeans and a T-shirt. It was a cold evening, but I'd be inside, so I chose a sweatshirt rather than my heavy jacket. As soon as Tang and Tilly had finished their dinner, I loaded them into the Jeep and headed toward town. Although neither Tony nor I lived in the incorporated area known as White Eagle, I lived on the south side of town and he lived on the mountain to the north, so it was necessary to pass through town when traveling from one residence to the other. As I passed Pike's Place, I found myself pulling into the parking lot. The bar was crowded this evening and I wasn't in the mood for a drink, but I had an urge to return to Pike's cabin one final time.

When I got out of my Jeep I found the front door unlocked. I turned the knob and quietly went inside. The cabin was dark except for a thin strip of light showing beneath the bedroom door. I walked slowly to the door and opened it. "Fantasia. What are you doing here?"

"I suppose I could ask you the same thing."

I looked around the room, noticing the furniture had been moved since the last time I was here. "I stopped by to check on things," I eventually answered. "But it seems you're looking for something."

"Whatever would I be looking for?" Fantasia laughed as she made her way to the doorway, where I was standing.

I could see she expected me to step aside to allow her to pass, but I held my ground. Suddenly everything was beginning to come together. "You killed Pike."

"What?" Fantasia tried to look shocked, but her acting left a lot to be desired. "Why on earth would I kill Pike?"

"Pike came to your home to speak to Austin about the secret of his birth. Amberley told me that you liked to snoop, so I imagine you overheard the conversation. You're a young, beautiful woman who's married to an old but rich man. It seems obvious Austin's money was the main attraction."

"Of course Austin's money was behind my interest in him. It's not against the law to marry for money."

"No, it's not. But when you found out Austin wasn't the child of Dillinger and Alberta Wade, you panicked. The only other person, as far as you knew, who knew the truth was Pike, so you borrowed Austin's car when he was out of town and killed him."

Fantasia's face hardened, but she didn't reply right away. When she spoke, she said bitterly, "What would you do if you married a man with one foot in the grave to secure your own financial security, only to find out he wasn't who you thought he was, that he might, after all was said and done, end up penniless?"

'I certainly wouldn't kill anyone."

"Pike knew Austin's secret, which made him a liability. If Austin's brothers found out he wasn't a Wade they'd probably disinherit him."

"They do know and they didn't."

Fantasia looked confused. "They know?"

"I spoke to Austin today and he told me that he'd shared his secret with his brothers when he returned from his trip."

Fantasia narrowed her gaze. "I saw you at the house earlier and figured you were there to discuss Austin's situation. I hoped you didn't know the truth, but I suppose if he let the cat out of the bag it really doesn't matter. I can't believe Austin would be foolish enough to take such a risk with my money."

"You mean his money," I countered.

"His, mine; they're one and the same now that we're married."

"I'm sure the Wade family trust is written in such a way as to ensure that gold diggers don't get much once their wealthy husbands die."

Fantasia raised a brow. "You think so?"

"I do. But I suppose it doesn't really matter because you're going to have a hard time spending Austin's money from prison."

Fantasia pulled a small handgun out of her jacket pocket. "I'm not going to prison. I found the button I realized had popped off my jacket when I was here, so once I kill you there won't be any evidence to show I was ever here."

"There are other people who saw Austin's car here the day Pike died."

"Austin's car, not mine."

"Someone will figure it out."

"Doubtful."

Fantasia lifted the gun and aimed it at my chest. I couldn't believe the crazy woman was actually going to shoot me. I did the only thing I could and ran toward her to tackle the gun from her hand. The gun went off and I felt a sharp stab of pain as I fell to the floor. Luckily, I landed on top of Fantasia, who hit her head on the way down. I rolled off her and checked for a pulse. She was alive but unconscious. I pulled my phone out of my pocket and dialed 911.

Chapter 10

Saturday, December 23

"I'm telling you, *Star Wars* figurines aren't considered to be acceptable tree ornaments," Bree argued as she tried to convince Shaggy to make room for the beautiful glass ornaments she'd brought. Bree, Shaggy, Tony, and I were having a friends' Christmas dinner tonight because we had plans with family over the holiday. Shaggy and Bree had called a truce and agreed to get along, at least for the moment, which made me deliriously happy.

It had been a rough few days. While the bullet had just grazed my side, it had still required an overnight stay at the hospital and leave from work until the stitches came out. I wasn't thrilled with all the sitting around, but Tony had been going out of his way to keep me occupied.

I'd adopted a black, longhaired kitten as a companion for Tang. She was a sweet little thing I'd named Tinder. I guess having some time at home to get the kittens used to each other was a good thing. Hopefully, once Tilly and I went back to work, Tang and Tinder would be perfectly happy to stay home and destroy my cabin.

Tang and Tinder were chasing each other around the room while Tilly and my Christmas present to Tony got to know each other. Brady had learned that the dog with the wounded paws had been on his own since his owner had died, so I decided a sweet and very intelligent German shepherd, whose name, I learned, was Titan, was exactly the sort of Christmas present Tony needed. I supposed I was taking a risk when I just showed up with the dog, but Tony seemed both shocked and delighted by my gift.

As for Pike's murder, Fantasia was in jail. I felt bad for Austin, but I was pretty sure he was better off without that gold-digging bimbo. While Tony and I hadn't answered all the questions we'd uncovered along our journey, we'd resolved a few. We still didn't know what Pike had been looking for when he'd visited the library, but Adam Weston had verified that his father had stolen Bloomfield's gold, and we now knew Bloomfield had been killed by a man whose wife he'd been sleeping with. White Eagle had been born of the sweat of men and women who'd dared to pit their wiliness against the elements, and after discovering some of the hardships our founding fathers had endured, I suspected there were more secrets buried with them.

"Considering Shaggy and Bree are playing nicely now, this should be a good time for me to give you your Christmas present," Tony said.

I smiled. "You got me something?"

"I did, but we'll need to go downstairs."

"Sounds mysterious, but I'm game."

Tony took my hand and led me down to the cellar. He closed the door and motioned for me to sit on the sofa. Once I was comfy he handed me a folder.

"What's this?"

"A clue."

My eyes got big. "A clue in the case we decided to abandon and never speak of again?"

Tony nodded. "Even though we agreed to put this mystery behind us, I'll admit I've been spending some of my free time on the puzzle we uncovered when we looked in to your father's death. I can't say I've found anything that would constitute an answer, but I might be getting somewhere after all these years."

"I thought you said I'd be better off leaving it alone."

"I did say that. And if you think that's best you don't need to open the folder."

I looked at it with uncertainty. I'd tried to put it all behind me, but I suppose I still wanted to know. I opened the folder to find a photo of my dad. He was standing near a wall with water behind it. I didn't recognize it, so I glanced at Tony.

"The photo was taken in Los Angeles. See this building here?" Tony pointed to a building in the background. "It was constructed ten years ago, after the building that had originally stood there was destroyed in a fire."

"Ten years ago? But my dad died thirteen years ago."

"You've said from the beginning there was something suspicious about not only your dad's death but his life before that. Unless your father had a twin, I'd say you were on to something."

To say I was shocked would be putting it mildly. From as far back as I could remember, my dad had been a long-haul trucker who was away from home most of the time, leaving me feeling unloved and deserted. At some point I'd begun to imagine that he hadn't abandoned me to deliver canned goods from one coast to the other, but rather was away from his family because of some superimportant role he played to ensure the safety of all humankind. Pretending my dad was a spy or superhero gave me comfort, so when I'd found the letter I was sure was a secret message, I'd taken it to Tony. To learn the letter had been nothing of the kind was disappointing, but I'd found I was still obsessed with finding out who my father was and whether he was really dead. The remains that had been delivered to my mother had consisted of little more than ash, so as far as I was concerned, unless I could prove otherwise, my dad was alive *and* dead. Tony had been drawn in by my story and agreed to help me. As time passed and every clue led to a dead end, Tony had encouraged me to let it go, to get on with my life. I'd tried to do that, but it appeared Tony hadn't given up on the project after all.

A tear slid down my cheek. Tony pulled me to my feet, gathered me into his arms, and hugged me. "I'm so sorry. I didn't mean to make you cry."

"No. It's okay. I want—no, I need to know the truth. But after so many years of chasing clues that ended up not being clues at all, I guess I'd mostly given up." I pulled back slightly so Tony and I were face-to-face, his nose less than an inch from mine.

"We need to find him. If he's alive, I need to know where he's been and why he deserted his family."

Tony used a finger to move a strand of my long hair from my cheek and tuck it behind my ear. "If your dad is alive I'll find him. If he's died in the years since this photo was taken, I'll find that out as well. But before I continue, I want you to be sure you're prepared to know the truth. Finding out what happened to your dad might not provide you with the comfort or closure you're looking for."

"You think he might not be the good guy I remember?"

"I think there are a lot of reasons a man may choose to disappear. Not all of them will be noble. Are you sure you want the truth, knowing it may not be what you want to hear?"

I nodded. "I'm sure."

"Okay. Then I'll keep looking. It only took me twelve years to find this photo; just imagine what I can do with another twelve," Tony said in a light voice that was meant to sound joking, though I knew he was quite serious.

"I know the answers I'm looking for are buried deep and I'm not expecting you to find my answers in a day, but it comforts me to know you're looking." I wasn't sure if my dad had left because he had an important role to play or if he'd simply grown bored and decided to carve out a new life, but whatever the reason for his departure from my life, I knew finding my answers was the only way I was going to be able to really move on from the mystery that had consumed my life for more than thirteen years.

Tony hugged me again, squeezing me so tightly I could barely breathe. I wasn't sure what he said, but it sounded like he was whispering to me in Italian. I guess I shouldn't be surprised. Tony's family was from Italy, but somehow, I'd never thought of him as being Italian.

"I guess we should go back up to make sure the kids are behaving themselves," Tony said before kissing me on the forehead and taking a step back.

"Are you talking about the four-legged kids or the human ones?"

"Both. I've prepared a delicious meal and I'd hate for it to end up on someone's head."

I felt a warmth in my heart as Tony and I returned upstairs to find Shaggy and Bree laughing as they looked through an old photo album, while both dogs and cats were watching from their pillows in front of the fire. For a brief moment I felt like we were almost a family, but knowing Bree and Shaggy, when the magic of Christmas passed they'd be back at each other's throats.

"I think your dogs are in love with each other," Shaggy commented.

"Yeah, I don't think Tilly is going to be happy when we leave," Bree seconded.

"They do look pretty content," Tony agreed.

"I guess we'll just have to get together more often so the dogs can visit," I said.

Tony smiled as he took my hand in his and led me to the kitchen, where the feast he'd prepared for us was waiting to be served. As I spooned green beans into a bowl, I gave a silent prayer of thanks for the magic of the holiday and the good friends I was blessed to share it with.

Coming 12/15/2017

Sneak Peek – Reindeer Roundup

Friday, December 15

I wasn't sure exactly when the fog had rolled in, but I was having the darnedest time trying to figure out where I was and what it was I was supposed to be doing. Even though the fog was so thick I couldn't clearly define the images surrounding me, I could see red and green blinking lights overhead. I closed my eyes as nausea gripped me. I tried to focus and figure out what was going on, but the sound of "Rudolph the Red-Nosed Reindeer" blaring through loudspeakers was so jolting it caused my head to pulsate in time to the music. I had pretty much convinced myself I was trapped in some sort of Christmas nightmare when I heard the voice of my best friend, Ellie Denton.

"Zoe, are you okay?"

I tried to focus on her voice, but it seemed so far away.

"Come on, sweetie. Wake up. The ambulance is on the way."

Ambulance? Maybe I really *was* trapped in a nightmare.

"I think she's coming to," Ellie assured someone as the fog began to lift. I realized I was lying on my back on a hard object. Maybe the floor. I didn't have a clear sense of where I was or how I'd come to be there, but I could feel Ellie's hands stroking my hair as I made my way through the murky landscape toward the voice that was pleading with me to open my eyes.

"She's opening her eyes," Ellie screeched.

I cringed. My head felt like I'd partied way too hard and Ellie's happy chirps of relief weren't helping.

"Are you okay?" Ellie's brown eyes looked directly into my blue ones. "Do you feel any pain?"

"I'm fine. What happened?"

"You tripped over the elf with the candy canes and fell face first into Santa's lap. You have a huge bump on your head, but I think the baby is okay."

Baby? I reached down and touched my swollen stomach. Oh God, Catherine. "Are you sure

Catherine's okay?" I croaked, barely able to find my voice.

"I think so. You tripped and fell to your knees. When you fell forward your face hit Santa's chair, but he caught you by the shoulders. You didn't hit your stomach. There's an ambulance on the way. Just lie still until it gets here.

As it turned out, lying still was all I felt up to, so I happily complied. I could hear people moving around, but it seemed like too much of an effort to open my eyes, so I simply allowed myself to drift into the space that exists between sleep and wakefulness. As I waited for whatever would come next, I let my mind wander wherever it chose in an attempt to block out the chaos around me.

I'd been Christmas shopping with Ellie and baby Eli. We'd been marveling at the lavish holiday decorations the department store had set out this year when Ellie noticed a Santa sitting in a big red chair listening to the wishes of the boys and girls who'd been waiting in line. Ellie wanted to get a photo of Eli with Santa, so we'd headed in that direction. I remembered being a little sad that Catherine wasn't with us this Christmas, while at the same time being excited about what the new year would bring. I remember being worried, but for the life of me I couldn't remember why. I do remember the fear in my heart had caused me to become distracted, which is probably how I tripped over the elf in the first place.

"The ambulance is here," someone said.

I could hear rustling and shuffling but decided it still wasn't worth the effort to open my eyes, so I just lay there and waited.

"The ambulance is going to take you to the hospital," Ellie said. "I can't go with you because I have Eli with me, but I called Levi and he's on his way. We'll meet you there."

"Zak?"

Ellie took my hand in hers. "Zak isn't here, sweetie. Remember the accident?"

I cringed as my eyes closed harder. Suddenly I remembered what it was I'd been distracted by.

******

I wasn't sure how long I'd been asleep, but when I next opened my eyes Ellie was sitting in the chair next to the bed I was lying in. I was hooked up to so many monitors I couldn't begin to figure out what they were measuring, but I felt a lot better, so I hoped everything was fine.

"Ellie?"

Ellie set down the book she'd been reading and smiled. "Oh good, you're awake."

"Is Catherine okay?"

"Catherine's fine. You are as well. The doctor said you have a mild concussion and he wants to keep an eye on you overnight, but you should be fine to go home tomorrow."

I put my hand on my stomach and was greeted with a strong kick. There was no doubt in my mind that my daughter was going to be a soccer player. "What about the kids?"

"Levi picked both Alex and Scooter up at school and took them home. Alex's working on the Santa's sleigh project and Scooter is finishing up a project for school. Levi, Eli, the dogs, and I are going to stay at your place for a few days. We don't want you to be alone while Zak's away."

"Does he know?"

Ellie shook her head. "I wanted to talk to you first. On one hand, Zak's your husband and should be informed of your little accident, but on the other, I felt like he already had a lot on his plate and didn't want to send him totally over the edge."

"I'm glad you waited to tell him. If you told him he'd only worry, and he really needs to focus on his mom right now. I'm fine, and with you and Levi to help me, I'm sure everything here in Ashton Falls will be back to normal in no time."

"Whatever you think is best. The doctor is on his way in to speak to you, so I'm going to go call Levi to let everyone back at the house know you're awake."

"Okay. And thanks, Ellie."

The doctor came in to do an exam as soon as Ellie left. I lay quietly, trying not to worry about my husband and the internal struggle we'd both been dealing with since we'd learned of his mother's accident. Any way you diced it, it was my fault Zak's mother was lying in a hospital in Paris, France, with serious injuries. No, I hadn't been driving the automobile that had run her down, but the only reason she was in Paris and not here, safe in Ashton Falls, was because she'd wanted to spend Christmas with us, I hadn't wanted her to, and Zak had wanted to make me happy. He knew reasoning with his mother wouldn't work, so he'd sent her to Paris for Christmas as some sort of a bribe.

Had there ever been a worse daughter-in-law than me?

"Are you feeling any pain?" the doctor asked.

"No. I'm fine."

"Your whole body just tensed up."

I let out a breath. "Sorry. I was just thinking about my mother-in-law. She was in a serious accident overseas and I guess I'm worried."

The doctor took off his gloves and took a step back. "That's understandable, but it's important that you try to relax. Your baby has been through enough stress for one day."

"I know. I'll try harder. Is everything okay?"

"Everything should be fine. I want to keep you overnight for observation, but you should be able to go home tomorrow. Your friend told me she'd be there to help you until your husband returned."

"She will. I'll have a lot of help."

"Okay, then. Get some rest and I'll check in on you in the morning."

I noticed my cell phone on the nightstand next to the bed. I picked it up and checked for messages. Although it was after six, I realized I hadn't checked my phone since before Ellie had picked me up for lunch and shopping. There were eight texts and two voice messages but nothing from Zak. I figured he should have landed in France by now and would have called, but I supposed he had more important things on his mind.

The first text message was from my mom, asking me if I had any news on Zak's mom. I texted her back, letting her know I hadn't heard anything, but I'd let her know as soon as I did. I considered telling her about my own elf accident, but I knew she'd just worry, so I decided to wait until I was safely home before mentioning anything about it.

The next text message was from a woman named Stella Green. I'd gone to high school with her, but we hadn't stayed in touch, so I didn't consider her to be a close friend. The text just said. "Call me," so I skipped it and went on to the next.

The third text was from the Christmas store in town, letting me know the custom ornaments I'd ordered had come in and I could pick them up at my earliest convenience. I was excited to see how they'd turned out, so maybe I'd ask Ellie to pick them up for me.

The fourth text was from Stella again, asking me to call her and adding the words, "it's really important" to the end. I once again skipped over it, figuring I'd call her after I got home.

The fifth text was from Scooter, asking if his friend Tucker could spend the night. I realized he'd texted before he knew I was in the hospital, but I decided to text back anyway, letting him know I was doing fine but he'd need to take a rain check.

The sixth text was from my grandfather's girlfriend, Hazel Hampton, asking if I was planning to participate in the cookie exchange this year. Knowing Ellie, she'd already made cookies for us both to bring, so I texted back to let her know I planned to attend and wanting to confirm that the exchange was still scheduled for Tuesday.

The seventh text was from my mom again, asking if I wanted her to make a Christmas stocking for Catherine. I texted back that Catherine wasn't due until three weeks after Christmas, but if she had time and wanted to do it, we could always use the stocking next year.

The last text was from Alex, asking if I was okay. I guess Levi must have told her what was going on. I told her I was fine, but they wanted to keep an eye on me, so I was staying the night. I told her I'd call her later.

Both voice messages were from Stella. The first said she'd been getting strange emails and she wondered if Zak could help her track down the source. The second message sounded a bit tenser, as she asked me to please get back to her right away. I was about to call her when Ellie came in.

"So, everything went well?" Ellie asked.

"Yes. I can go home tomorrow. You don't have to stay with me. Go home to your husband and baby. I'll be fine."

"I know you'll be fine, but I'm not leaving until they kick me out." Ellie noticed the phone in my hand. "He didn't call?"

I shook my head. "He must hate me."

Ellie sat down on the side of my bed and took my hand in hers. "Zak doesn't hate you. He loves you. It's not your fault his mother was in an accident."

"If I hadn't been such a big, complaining baby she'd be safe and sound in Ashton Falls, making me crazy and not clinging to her life halfway around the world."

"You might not have wanted her to come to Ashton Falls for Christmas, but you didn't force her to go to Paris, and you certainly didn't force her to walk down a narrow street late at night where a drunk driver ran into her. Why was she walking down a narrow street late at night anyway?"

"I don't know. Zak doesn't know. It is rather odd."

"To be honest, Zak's mother doesn't seem the sort to walk anywhere."

"She's not. The whole thing makes no sense. Hopefully, she'll regain consciousness and tell us what happened."

Ellie squeezed my hand. "She will. She may already have. Chances are, Zak hasn't even made it to the hospital yet. I'm sure he'll call you when he has news to share."

I wanted to respond that I was sure he would, but I really wasn't so sure. I couldn't get out of my mind the haunted look on his face when he'd first received the call from the hospital in Paris. He'd looked so lost and scared. I wasn't used to my big, strong husband looking like a terrified little boy. I closed my eyes, fighting back my own tears.

"Are you okay? Should I call the nurse?"

"I'm just tired, and I can't help but worry about Zak and his mom. Let's talk about something else. Did Levi have a chance to talk to the guy who's running the new tree lot in town?"

"He tried, but the guy's being completely unreasonable. Despite the fact that his lot is directly next door to the one Levi's running for the high school sports program, he maintains it's his right to sell his trees for whatever price he wants even though it's killing the high school's business."

"What I don't understand is how he's selling the trees so cheaply."

"It seems like he's using the cheap trees to get people onto the lot and then he sells them baked goods, ornaments, photos with Santa, and a variety of other add-ons for an exorbitant price. Levi's getting pretty frustrated, and I hear he's not the only one who's complained about the loud music and flashing lights, but it appears he has permits for everything, so there isn't a lot Levi can do."

"Poor Levi. It's really going to hurt the high school if they can't sell their trees."

"Yeah." Ellie sighed. "It really is. But I don't want you to worry about that or anything else. The doctor said you need to relax."

"It's kinda hard to relax with so much going on."

Ellie put her hand over mine. "I know, sweetie. But you need to try. If not for yourself, for Catherine."

Ellie was right. The past twenty-four hours had been so hectic, and I knew I needed to create a safe and stress-free environment for Catherine, so I tried to focus on happy thoughts. "The ornaments I ordered are ready at the holiday store. I don't suppose you'd mind picking them up on your way home?"

"I'd be happy to. And I love the idea of a custom ornament for each member of your family. I wish I'd thought of it, but it's probably too late to order them now."

"I was going to surprise you, but I ordered ornaments for you, Levi, Eli, and even Shep and Karloff."

Ellie's face softened. "Sweetie, that's so nice. Thank you so much."

"In addition to the ornaments I ordered for your family and mine, I also got ornaments for my parents and Harper," I said, referring to my sister, "as well as my grandpa and Hazel."

"I'm sure everyone will love them. It means a lot that you remembered us."

"I figured I'm not good at cooking or baking like you are and I can't sew like Mom can, but I can shop with the best of them and I wanted to do something special this year."

"Well, I'm excited to see what you got."

"Speaking of cooking and baking, Hazel texted me about the cookie exchange on Tuesday. I'm assuming you've made or will make cookies for both of us?"

"I'm totally on it. And we can go together, so you don't need to drive."

"Thanks, El. You're a good friend."

"I'm just trying to be as good a friend as my best friend."

I frowned. "You do mean me?"

"Of course, silly. By the way, the kids and I plan to finish decorating tomorrow, if it's okay with you. I don't want to intrude on your space, but I figured you probably wouldn't feel up to hanging the garland from the staircase or finishing the Santa's Village Zak was working on for the front lawn before he left."

"You're right. I probably won't be able to do it myself, but it would be nice to have everything done before Zak gets back. Alex knows where the garland for the stairs is stored and Zak had everything for the Santa's village in his shed. Oh, and tell Levi not to forget to feed the reindeer. I know Zak went over everything with him before he left."

Zak had rented eight reindeer for the Hometown Christmas event that would be held from five p.m. on December 22 until five p.m. on December 24. The reindeer were in a pen on our property for the time being, but the event committee planned to truck them to a pen near the Santa's Village, which was currently being erected for the annual event.

"I'll make sure Levi feeds them using the notes Zak left. I don't want you to worry about anything. Levi and I will take care of everything."

"Thanks, Ellie. I feel like I should be home taking care of things, not lying here doing nothing."

"The kids will be fine. The house will be fine."

"I know. It's just such a busy time at the Zimmerman household. Tell Alex the check Zak left for her shopping trip with the Santa's sleigh committee this weekend is in the top drawer of Zak's desk. I think they plan to go to the mall in Bryton Lake tomorrow to pick up whatever wish lists items weren't donated."

"I'll tell her. And don't worry. I have the impression Alex and her team have the whole thing handled."

"I'm sure they do."

"You look tired."

"I guess I am."

"Then I'm going to go and let you get some sleep. I'll be back in the morning."

"Okay. And thanks again."

As I closed my eyes in an attempt to fall asleep, I tried to focus on all the good things in my life. My wonderful husband and three honorary children. Pi was Zak's ward, or at least he had been before he turned eighteen. Currently, he was more of an assistant and would work full time for Zak once he finished college. He planned to come home for Christmas once he finished his last final on Wednesday. Scooter was thirteen and had first come to us when Zak agreed to babysitting duty after his mother died. Eventually, Scooter had come to live with us as well, and on a magical Christmas three years ago he'd brought with him his best friend, Alex, who had captured my heart the way no other child ever had. Alex was a brilliant and mature thirteen-year-old with a heart as big as creation. Last year she'd founded the Santa's sleigh program, collecting toys and food products for those in need and then distributed wrapped gifts and food baskets a few days before Christmas.

And then, of course, there were the four-legged members of the Donovan-Zimmerman household. My dog Charlie, Zak's dog Bella, Scooter's dog Digger, and my cats, Marlow and Spade. Alex seemed to have a revolving door of animals she fostered but right now all the animals that were in her care had found forever homes.

And last but not least, I was blessed with the best friends in the entire world, Levi and Ellie. They'd been my friends for most of my life and I considered them family. As I drifted off to sleep, my thoughts changed to baby Catherine, who would soon make her entrance into the world. I didn't say so to Ellie, but even though Catherine wasn't due until the middle of January I'd gone ahead and bought an ornament for her just in case she decided to make an early appearance. I'd been having a few contractions in the past week and the doctor has assured me Catherine was fully developed, so if she did decide to arrive a couple of weeks early everything should be fine. It was strange, because part of me was anxious for her arrival and another was terrified.

Recipes

Gingerbread—submitted by Pam Curran

Scottish Shortbread—submitted by Vivian Shane

Cranberry Jell-O Salad—submitted by Nancy Farris

Christmas Sugar Cookies—submitted by Darla Taylor

Gingerbread

Submitted by Pam Curran

This recipe came from my mother. She was such a sweet eater, so a lot of the recipes I have from her are sweets.

½ cup shortening
2½ cups flour
½ cup sugar
1½ tsp. baking soda
1 egg
1 tsp. cinnamon
1 cup molasses
1 tsp. ginger
1 cup hot water

Mix the above ingredients together. Bake in a 350-degree oven for about 45 minutes. Great with whipped cream on top.

Scottish Shortbread

Submitted by Vivian Shane

You'll need a shortbread mold for this recipe; I use a Hearthstone stoneware shortbread mold, but there are many different types on the market to choose from.

1½ cups sifted flour
¾ cup confectioner's sugar
¼ tsp. salt
½ lb. butter

Preheat oven to 325 degrees.

Mix all ingredients together, cutting butter into small pieces, and knead until the consistency becomes doughy, like piecrust. Press very firmly into mold, making sure the dough fits into every part of the surface. Place filled mold in oven and bake for 1 hour, until golden. Cool on rack before removing from mold. Dust confectioner's sugar over top.

Cranberry Jell-O Salad

Submitted by Nancy Farris

Christmas dinner at the Coopers' always included a cranberry Jell-O salad. This is one of my favorites!

1 can (20-oz.) crushed pineapple, undrained
2 small pkgs. raspberry gelatin
1 can (16-oz.) whole berry cranberry sauce
1 Granny Smith apple, chopped
⅔ cup chopped walnuts, optional

Drain pineapple into 4-cup measuring cup, reserving juice. Add enough cold water to juice to measure 3 cups. Pour into saucepan and bring to boil. Remove from heat and add dry Jell-O. Stir 2 minutes or until dissolved. Stir in cranberry sauce. Pour into large bowl. Refrigerate 90 minutes or until slightly thickened.

Stir in pineapple, chopped apple, and walnuts.

Refrigerate 4 hours or until firm.

Note: After you stir in the pineapple, apple, and walnuts, you can put it in a 9-x-13 pan until firm. Then cut in squares to serve on fancy salad plates. Top with a dollop of whipped cream.

Makes 14 servings, ½ cup each

Christmas Sugar Cookies

Submitted by Darla Taylor

2 cups all-purpose flour
2 tsp. baking powder (double recipe ~ 1 tbs. plus 1 tsp.)
½ tsp. salt (if you use a coarse salt it will need to be ground before measuring)
2 large eggs
1 cup sugar
¾ cup vegetable oil
2 tsp. vanilla extract
Red sugar sprinkles for topping
Hershey's Holiday Kisses Candy Cane Mint Candies

Stir flour, baking powder, and salt into a medium bowl and mix well.
Whisk eggs in a large bowl until blended. Add sugar, oil, and extract. Mix well.
Stir the dry ingredients into the egg mixture until blended.
Chill, covered, for at least 30 minutes. (I've left in the refrigerator overnight).

Preheat the oven to 400 degrees.
Prepare a small bowl of sugar and a small bowl of water.
Drop the cookie dough by rounded teaspoonfuls onto ungreased cookie sheets.

Dip a flat-bottomed glass into the water, then into the sugar, and use the sugared glass to flatten each cookie; I'm usually able to flatten two cookies for each dip; then this step will need to be repeated. Sprinkle the colored sugar onto the cookies to your taste.

Bake until lightly browned, about 6 to 8 minutes. When cookies come out of the oven, press an unwrapped Candy Cane Mint in the middle of each cookie; hint ~ it helps to have the candies unwrapped beforehand; tip ~ due to the white chocolate, these won't harden completely like milk or dark chocolate. Cool the cookies on baking sheets for about a minute, then move them to wire racks.

Alternate: You might try adding ½ tsp. mint extract to the cookie dough.

Yields about 2 dozen

Books by Kathi Daley

Come for the murder, stay for the romance.

Zoe Donovan Cozy Mystery:

Halloween Hijinks
The Trouble With Turkeys
Christmas Crazy
Cupid's Curse
Big Bunny Bump-off
Beach Blanket Barbie
Maui Madness
Derby Divas
Haunted Hamlet
Turkeys, Tuxes, and Tabbies
Christmas Cozy
Alaskan Alliance
Matrimony Meltdown
Soul Surrender
Heavenly Honeymoon
Hopscotch Homicide
Ghostly Graveyard
Santa Sleuth
Shamrock Shenanigans
Kitten Kaboodle
Costume Catastrophe
Candy Cane Caper
Holiday Hangover
Easter Escapade
Camp Carter
Trick or Treason
Reindeer Roundup

Tj Jensen Paradise Lake Mysteries by Henery Press:

Pumpkins in Paradise
Snowmen in Paradise
Bikinis in Paradise
Christmas in Paradise
Puppies in Paradise
Halloween in Paradise
Treasure in Paradise
Fireworks in Paradise
Beaches in Paradise – *June 2018*

Whales and Tails Cozy Mystery:

Romeow and Juliet
The Mad Catter
Grimm's Furry Tail
Much Ado About Felines
Legend of Tabby Hollow
Cat of Christmas Past
A Tale of Two Tabbies
The Great Catsby
Count Catula
The Cat of Christmas Present
A Winter's Tail
The Taming of the Tabby
Frankencat
The Cat of Christmas Future
The Cat of New Orleans – *February 2018*

Seacliff High Mystery:

The Secret
The Curse
The Relic
The Conspiracy
The Grudge
The Shadow
The Haunting

Sand and Sea Hawaiian Mystery:

Murder at Dolphin Bay
Murder at Sunrise Beach
Murder at the Witching Hour
Murder at Christmas
Murder at Turtle Cove
Murder at Water's Edge
Murder at Midnight

Writers' Retreat Southern Seashore Mystery:

First Case
Second Look
Third Strike
Fourth Victim
Fifth Night – *January 2018*

Rescue Alaska Paranormal Mystery:

Finding Justice

A Tess and Tilly Mystery:
The Christmas Letter

Road to Christmas Romance:
Road to Christmas Past

USA Today best-selling author **Kathi Daley** lives with her husband, kids, grandkids, and Bernese mountain dogs in beautiful Lake Tahoe. When she isn't writing, she likes to read (preferably at the beach or by the fire), cook (preferably something with chocolate or cheese), and garden (planting and planning, not weeding). She also enjoys spending time on the water when she's not hiking, biking, or snowshoeing the miles of desolate trails surrounding her home.

Kathi uses the mountain setting in which she lives, along with the animals (wild and domestic) that share her home, as inspiration for her cozy mysteries.

Kathi is a top 100 mystery writer for Amazon and won the 2014 award for both Best Cozy Mystery Author and Best Cozy Mystery Series.

She currently writes eight series: Zoe Donovan Cozy Mysteries, Whales and Tails Island Mysteries, Sand and Sea Hawaiian Mysteries, Writers' Retreat Southern Mysteries, Tj Jensen Paradise Lake Mysteries, Rescue Alaska Paranormal Mysteries, Tess and Tilly Cozy Mystery, and Seacliff High Teen Mysteries.

Giveaway:

I do a giveaway for books, swag, and gift cards every week in my newsletter, *The Daley Weekly*
http://eepurl.com/NRPDf

Other links to check out:
Kathi Daley Blog – publishes each Friday
http://kathidaleyblog.com
Webpage – **www.kathidaley.com**

Facebook at Kathi Daley Books –
www.facebook.com/kathidaleybooks

Kathi Daley Books Group Page –
https://www.facebook.com/groups/5695788231468 50/

E-mail – **kathidaley@kathidaley.com**

Goodreads –
https://www.goodreads.com/author/show/7278377. Kathi_Daley

Twitter at Kathi Daley@kathidaley –
https://twitter.com/kathidaley

Amazon Author Page –
https://www.amazon.com/author/kathidaley

BookBub –
https://www.bookbub.com/authors/kathi-daley

Pinterest – **http://www.pinterest.com/kathidaley/**

Made in the USA
Coppell, TX
11 December 2020